D1281448

HAPPY DAYS, UNCLE SERGIO

HAPPY DAYS, UNCLE SERGIO

MAGALI GARCÍA RAMIS

TRANSLATED BY
CARMEN C. ESTEVES

WHITE PINE PRESS · FREDONIA, NEW YORK

Publication of this book was made possible, in part,
by grants from the National Endowment for the Arts
and the New York State Council on the Arts.

Translator's Acknowledgements:
First of all, I would like to thank Magali García Ramis for her
trust, patience and encouragement, and for the friendship that
has evolved from this project.
Special thanks to my husband, James Kraus, and to a dear
friend, Lizabeth Paravisini-Gebert, for their careful reading of
the manuscript and valuable suggestions.
Thanks to the Professional Staff Congress of the City
University of New York for the grant to work on this translation.
And last but not least, thanks to Marjorie Agosín and Dennis
Maloney, whose vision has made possible the Secret Weaver
Series.

Book design by Elaine LaMattina

Cover painting: Nick Quijano

Manufactured in the United States of America

ISBN 1-877727-52-0

First printing 1995

9 8 7 6 5 4 3 2

White Pine Press • 10 Village Square • Fredonia, New York

To my husband, Jim,
for your warm hands next to mine.

To my daughter, Amanda,
to help you understand.

— Carmen C. Esteves

HAPPY DAYS, UNCLE SERGIO

To my brothers, José and Gerardo.

— Magali García Ramis

HAPPY DAYS, UNCLE SERGIO

The joyful days of love will never return.
                    Traditional Puerto Rican *Danza*

And his mother said to Boabdil, the last Moorish king of Granada, "You cry like a child for what you did not know how to defend as a man," a saying they repeated to us as children, every time we showed the slightest hint of cowardice.

It was not that my mother was not feminine, but that she liked to stand on one leg like a royal egret. Everyday, as the sun was setting, they used to take us for a walk along the seashore and we'd end up on the beach across from the old San Gerónimo fortress, looking towards the horizon, under palm trees and Australian pines and Mami would stand on one foot, with the other resting on her knee, and the two of us, imitating her, would challenge the world, good manners, and the family, balancing ourselves on one leg only, standing behind her in a row, like egrets in a documentary film.

My aunts Elena and Sara F. would ask her not to stand there like that — it didn't look nice; it wasn't ladylike — and she would shrug her shoulders to show she didn't care, and then she'd say that it was more comfortable like that and laugh. Ritually, every time my aunts scolded her, she would answer: "Oh my dears, I'm a little too old to be told what to do." And that was our favorite reply, because if there was something my brother and I longed for it was to be able to answer back when scolded and given advice, to finish growing up, and to get away forever from the life we were leading.

It was in the times of Muñoz Marín. It was a time of hope that still smelled like new. It was a time of razing red clay mountains to build houses in suburbs, of dissecting every green mountain with asphalt roads, of blossoming cement and hotels, of inaugurating dams and electric power stations, and of waiting in the new airport, that one day would be international, for the arrival of Americans dressed in iridescent gray suits, whom my uncle Roberto had to pick up as the representative of Fomento, the government development corporation. It was a time when we were islanders, and the sea, on every side the sea, was our only frontier. We lived surrounded by water and submerged in family tradition. And we had always been good, my brother and I. We ran in the solitude of our house, playing with American toy soldiers, Spanish decks of cards, and with dreams of leaving forever. We were growing up in the brightness of Puerto Rican mornings and in the shadow of the trees that shaded houses full of shadows in the stupor of identical and tranquil afternoons of Santurce in the fifties.

Mornings went by quickly, in school during the school year or playing when we were on vacation, but in the afternoons, around two o'clock, when Mami, Aunt Ele and Sara F. returned to their jobs and Nati had not come back from San Juan, we were always on the front porch watching the people who ventured out under the terrible sun, listening from afar to the kids on the street playing all the dangerous games in the world — street, kids, and world forbidden to us — and keeping an eye out for Margara.

Margara would walk by our street with a surly face, but everyone would turn to look at her. In the Dos Hermanos Bar and Grocery Store on the corner, the men would stick their heads out the door to whistle and yell, "Baby, you're sure looking good!" The women on their way to the market would lift their eyes to glance at her "mind-your-own-business" cat-like face with its intense gaze. They had explained to us that Margara was a woman who enjoyed walking the streets, a bad woman, and we understood, without really understanding, that she did things we couldn't even begin to imagine.

We never went near her, but that afternoon of mild sunlight my brother, my cousin Quique, and I were just too bored. And something occurred to us, and we whispered under our breath to see which one of us would dare, but they were all talk, so I, show-off that I was, stood up and yelled just as she was passing our gate, "Good-bye Margara," and then I was overcome by that terrible and devastating cold you feel when you have just done what you know to be prohibited from time immemorial, and I froze.

The three of us could not move; we held on to the gate and almost lost our breaths when she stopped, turned, and took a few steps towards us. I grabbed a fern, squeezed it, and crushed it in my hand. Out of the corner of my eye I saw Andrés' elbow next to mine, noticed how dirty it was, swallowed hard, felt hot, itchy, panicky. Margara was facing us. We had never seen her so close. We had never noticed her face so beautiful, her almond eyes, her pouting lips, her womanly scent, already identified by us as the scent of a lower-class woman.

But she was not looking at me or at Andrés, only at Quique who was so pretty everyone always looked at him. It was because he had blue eyes and curly, blondish hair, and on this side of the world they always said that people with that coloring were prettier. Margara reached over the wooden gate, touched his cheek and looked at Quique with tenderness. Quique smiled because he was so scatterbrained he didn't realize the danger he was in. From the corner grocery store, and who knows from how many balconies, they were looking at us. I dug my elbow into Andrés, since he was the oldest and it was up to him to save us all, and then he finally said: "Quique, get in the house, come on, let's go."

"Yes, let's go," I added. And he looked at us as if he had understood, and the three of us ran into the house. We closed the door, raised a corner of the door's lace curtain and saw that she had walked on.

Then we ran and locked ourselves in the bathroom. "Wash your face," Andrés told him. "You never know what diseases you might catch from those people." I said nothing.

At that moment, through the bathroom window that opened onto the back veranda, Mauricia, the cat, came in to drink water from the toilet, and I picked her up and began to pet her. Quique turned on the faucet, and we let the water run for a long time to calm ourselves. The three of us washed our hands and faces, drank some water, and began to breathe more easily. Andrés became serious. "You'll see how they're going to scold us. What's more, something will happen to us," he said. And I did not answer because I knew it was true, that even if you were sorry, when you did something wrong, punishment was sure to follow. Something bad was going to happen to us. And, as always, I was to blame; as always, I tried to fool all of us.

"No one saw us. No one will say anything. She won't say anything." But not even I believed it.

"You didn't have to call out to her," screamed Andrés. "We hadn't voted on that."

It was true. In our secret and democratic society, The Apaches of the Night, we used to vote before making decisions that affected the three of us. And we began to fight.

"What's going on in there? What're you doing in there? How dare you lock the door? Open up right away." It was our grandmother, Mamá Sara. We were in trouble. If there was one thing forbidden in our public life it was to speak to strangers, but if there was one thing forbidden in our private lives it was to lock ourselves in a room, especially the bathroom. "Didn't you hear me? Open up right now or I'll get a switch from the orange tree, and you'll really get what's coming to you!"

But we did not give her a chance to say anything else. We jumped out the window onto the veranda with Mauricia, went down to the backyard, took the little ladder from the side of the henhouse, put it close to the pigeon cage, climbed onto the cage's roof and lifted up the ladder. We stayed there the entire afternoon under the branches of the loquat tree.

The crucial thing was to remember to get down at some point before ten minutes after five to open the bathroom so that Mami or the aunts would not find it locked. As for Mamá Sara, Andrés said that she was old and, although she would tell, she would forget half of it as the afternoon went by, and Micaela, the maid, would not squeal on us, so she wouldn't be a problem. Andrés and Quique started to play jacks and I petted Mauricia holding her against her will, close enough to hear her purring, while I felt a terrible urge to cry, to finally grow up, to leave that place.

This is more or less how I remember the eve of his arrival, hidden, as I would always be, fleeing from the punishment for the rules I went on breaking, one after another, unintentionally, petting cats and growing up in fear, afraid of so many things, before he arrived. Where was he that day? Walking the streets around Riverside Drive? On the way to his lover's house? Returning to the company the volumes he did not sell from their collection of Famous Men, hating those abominable pasteurized half-true versions of history — Washington never told a lie, the Sun-King was admirable because he built Versailles, Cortés brought true religion and civilization to México — while anguished and unfulfilled, he carried under his arm a book of poems by Miguel Hernández?

The next day Daruel could not be found. We looked for him all over the neighborhood, but there was no trace of him. I understood right away that this was the punishment: fatal, conclusive, just, exactly what would hurt me most. We looked and looked for him as if he were going to appear, but I knew he would never show up again. "Don't worry about the cat," Micaela told us. "He's after a female, and he'll return with his tail between his legs to sleep for three straight days."

But he did not come back. Daruel was the only cat with his own name in our house, and he was half mine. All the others were named Mauricio or Mauricia because Mamá Sara said those were cat names. All the nine or fourteen or whatever number we had at any time, until Aunt Ele would grab two or three, put them in a bag and head for Carolina to set them free near a dairy. "There they'll be taken care off and given milk because they'll drive mice away," she would say if she saw us worried about the abandoned cats.

But Daruel was ours; we had picked him up outside church one Sunday. I wanted to name him Manuel for a Spanish singer I had fallen in love with when I was four years old. Andrés wanted to name him Darío because he had just read the biography of the Persian king defeated by Alexander the Great and was very impressed. But they told us that under no circumstance could we name an animal after a person, that it was disrespectful, so we settled on Daruel and pampered and loved him a lot. Sara F. always predicted that he would be stolen because he was so beautiful. And then, as punishment for my disobedience, he disappeared.

At six in the afternoon in the midst of a light rain, Andrés and I sat on the steps in front of the house without saying a word. We both knew we had lost Daruel, but we did not want to say it. It was getting dark — it is always getting dark when important people arrive in your life — when a taxi pulled up and stopped in front of our gate. The driver got out and placed a very large old suitcase and two or three boxes tied with rope on the sidewalk. From the back of the car a tall man dressed in a brown striped suit and Panama hat got out. He paid the driver and just stood there, looking at our house. His enormous eyes with long, feminine eyelashes studied the walls, the floorboards, the windows and the trees that grew so close to the house that they partially hid it. And then he stared at us. It was obvious that he was shy with those he didn't know, like us, and although he looked like us, he was a stranger so I screamed, "MAMIIII, COME HERE!"

Mami opened the door and light from the house poured out, illuminating us but not the man. "What're you doing out there getting wet? Come in right now; it's dark already. What's the matter?" she rattled off her questions and commands without stopping to breathe. Then she saw the man and changed her tone and assumed her lady-of-the house, show-me-some-respect tone: "Do you want something? Can I help you?" She saw the suitcase. She looked again at the man. She moved close to us. "Oh my God! Sergio? Sergio! SERGIO! Mamá, Elena, Sergio, Sara, come, it's Sergio; Sergio's back!" My uncle Sergio had returned home.

That night was like a party. We phoned the entire family, and Aunt Clara and Uncle Roberto were the first to arrive. Then Cousin Germánico came alone because Aunt Rosa could not find anyone to leave the girls with, and even Aunt Meri and Uncle Vicente came from Guaynabo. Uncle Sergio was introduced to all the kids because none of us remembered him, even though he said he had seen the three older ones when we were babies. Mamá Sara was embracing him and smiling with her sixty-four teeth, as my family would say.

We had inherited her big and perfectly aligned teeth, and with them we now forced our smiles. Mamá Sara made me kiss him on the cheek, since I never wanted to kiss anyone, and to my embarrassed surprise his jacket smelled so good and his cheek was so soft, and his scent, especially around his neck, was so appealing. And my kiss was so quick and his so sweet that even though Daruel did not appear that night, I did not think about him until the next day.

The first thing we asked Mami the next day was why didn't Uncle Sergio let us know beforehand of his arrival so we could pick him up at the airport since one of our favorite family vocations was to go in hordes to meet or say good-bye to everyone each time they traveled. "Well, we couldn't go to the airport because he came by boat," answered Mami in a mocking tone.

That day I had no patience. "Well, then to the docks. Why didn't he notify us?" I said it curiously and impatiently, bordering on the sassiness they had struggled to purge from me since birth.

"I don't know why," Mami pointed out and immediately she scolded me. "And don't you go asking him anything either. Maybe he wanted to surprise us, or he was in a rush when he left and he couldn't let us know. Whatever it was, it's none of your business. And now that we're on this subject, I want to make this very clear to both of you. I don't want you bothering him or snooping around his room or asking him questions about what's none of your business. He's a man, and men aren't meant to be followed around with questions about what they do or don't do."

He was a man, and for all we could remember from our lives, we had always lived among women. Despite the visits of Uncle Roberto, Cousin Germánico or Auntie Meri's husband, Uncle Vicente, in our everyday world everything was organized, decided and carried out by women.

Aunt Ele, the oldest, made all the decisions — from what color we would paint the house to where we would go on vacation. She was a doctor, like my grandfather, and she hoped that both Andrés and I would follow in her footsteps. María Angélica, my mother, decided everything that concerned the two of us, and when she married my father Gustavo, the second child of the Solís, she came to live in my paternal grandparents' house. When my father died in the war, Andrés and I were very young and they all decided that the three of us would live with them forever. Marí A., as my aunts called her, was a nurse, and had studied with Aunt Clara; that's how she met Papi. We loved to listen to her story of how they met in the Presbiteriano Hospital when they collided with each other at a hallway corner, and she swooned when she saw how handsome my father was. I could not remember him, neither could Andrés, but he lied and told his friends that he did.

My mother looked so much like my aunts that she was more like their sister than their sister-in-law. Only her sense of humor distinguished her from the Solís family. Along with my mother and Aunt Ele was Sara Fernanda, my other aunt, who was a secretary and adored the cinema and would take us as often as she could to all movies rated A-1, suitable for families, by the Catholic code. She worked for the Department of Health, was the best driver of all, the best seamstress and embroiderer, and the one who traveled every time she saved some money.

There was also Cousin Nati Machado, a relative of my grandmother's, brought up by Mamá Sara as her own, who worked as a technician at the Department of Tropical Medicine, and who, every time she could, brought home a projector and several movies to entertain us in the evenings. The movies were about germs, all kinds of germs, bacteria and organisms that caused infections. They used them to educate the community but she would show them as if they were straight from Hollywood. From the movies that Cousin Nati brought home, we learned all the bad things that could happen to people who picked up things from the ground, walked barefoot in the tropics, or put their hands in their mouths.

Above them all, and far above us, reigned Mamá Sara. Mamá Sara had a chair with a high back, like a queen, that she would place at the head of the dining room table, and she insisted on keeping the chair opposite her's empty, so that the Man, depending on who was visiting — Uncle Roberto, Monsignor Serrano, or even Cousin Germánico — could sit in it. Mamá Sara wore black, white or lilac. She raised hens and pigeons in the yard and canaries in the house. Mamá Sara played with memories that little by little were getting confused and sometimes called my brother Andrés "Sergio" because it seemed to her that the boy jumping around the house in short pants was her youngest son. Mamá Sara talked to her canaries and covered their cages one by one with mosquito nets, cut and sewn to fit, so that the evening mosquitoes would not make them sick.

With her hair gathered in a yellowish gray bun and her wide hips swaying down the halls to the slow rhythm of someone who is soon departing, she dominated with her spirit our manless family.

Mamá Sara had a maid, Micaela, who had been with us only a few years, but she had been recommended by Eloísa, the woman who raised my aunts, and for that reason Mamá kept her, although she scolded her almost daily because in the afternoons she would stay in front of the house, talking with the other maids from the neighborhood or with the boyfriends who whistled for her to go out.

My other aunts were married. Aunt María — Auntie Meri — was married to a very quiet man, Uncle Vicente. They only liked to grow plants and had a house in Guaynabo, in the countryside, on the outskirts of the city, and everyday they went to their government jobs — I really did not know where — and from there back to their house to plant, water and trim their garden, and we only saw them at family parties. The other one, Auntie Clara, was Quique's mother. Quique was like our brother and he stayed with us during the day. She was married to Uncle Roberto, who worked for the Fomento Development Corporation, and every afternoon she would come in her Buick to get Quique. Her two other sons were Germán Andrés, who was almost the same age as Andrés, and Robertito who was very young. They attended San Jorge School near their home, but Fernando Enrique, Quique, was enrolled in our school because Mamá Sara took care of him when he was a baby and Auntie Clara began to work and she became very attached to that grandson and had to see him everyday.

We didn't like Germán Andrés at all because he always teased us about the fact that he had a father and we did not, that his father had a very important position, and that he was given more allowance money than we were. When he visited our house we sized one another up like alley cats, at a distance, moving around the house looking askance at each other, until, in some corner of the house, we pounced. He fought dirty, but Andrés was the strongest of all of us, so he always won. Quique did not fight, and we knew that all of this upset him because Germán was his brother, but we could not avoid fighting. Sometimes I would bite Germán and gain a bit of respect. His father, Uncle Roberto, came for lunch sometimes, but in our daily lives there had never been a man who would establish his masculine rhythm and way of life in our world.

Up till then our world had been defined, measurable and perfect. It covered twenty square blocks, from bus stop 20 to bus stop 15 along Ponce de León Avenue, the most important thoroughfare in those days. It had a market, government buildings, banks, coffee shops, churches, schools, pastry shops, and nine movie houses, but the irreplaceable store for us was the Atenas Drugstore where every Wednesday Andrés and I waited impatiently for the arrival of a new shipment of comic books. We used to buy the latest adventures of Tarzan, Black Hawk, Wonder Woman, The Fox and the Crow, and *Adventures from Real Life, Exemplary Lives*, and *Legends from America*. After the Catholic Archdioceses, the Novaro

Publishing House in México was the most important influence in our upbringing. At the Atenas Drugstore we would stock up on comics and we would buy all other indispensable things: three-cent candies, Royal Crown and Grape Soda, plastic ships to assemble and magic knives that had a spring that hid the plastic blade so it really looked like your knife was piercing the skin of enemies you stabbed. These were our favorite props when we performed the rituals of the Apaches of the Night Society, before we attacked the pale faces.

Ours was a world of familiar and unchangeable smells, tastes and rituals where every afternoon we could breathe the aroma of Mamá Sara's fresh brewed coffee, where lemonade was made daily for our afternoon snack, and where the front door never had to be locked because someone was always inside waiting for you. We had Tamaqui, a female, Majorcan sheep dog, since everything that had some connection to Spain was preferable to all else, who every year, without fail, had puppies so that we could play with them. Every few months there was a sunny Sunday visit to the Spanish ships docked in the harbor, where Mamá Sara bought the yellow, white and orange canaries that filled our house. They brought them in the ship's galleys, and you needed to go up and down many stairs to arrive there. Andrés and I would try to escape from the family to sneak into places where we were not allowed, but some sailor would always catch us and take us back to the deck.

Life was simply measured by schooldays, vacations and religious holidays. During Christmas they always took us to El Yunque, the rain forest, to walk the trails and to eat next to cold streams that seemed to come from the bowels of the earth. In summer they would take us to beaches all around the island. And during Lent, since it was a tradition in my family to dress the altars of Christ the Redeemer Church, they would take us out of school for a few days and recruit us to tie hundreds of flowers to little wooden sticks that we would hand to Mami and my aunts. They would then shape them as chalices, angels and rays of light, all made from white, yellow and lilac chrysanthemums, daisies, red carnations, purple irises, all riveted with little green branches of *café de l'India*.

On Holy Thursday we would arrive at Church and were allowed to walk where it was forbidden to all but altar boys to help fill the naves with flowers in celebration of the mystery of the Eucharist, of God's transubstantiation. We were allowed to go to the sacristy where we would help Mami and Nati take, from enormous drawers, the robes belonging to Monsignor Serrano and the other four parish priests in order to examine them and prepare them for the solemn holidays. The robes, made with gold thread, had been patched by maids. "Look at this. How awful," Nati would say, and we would take them home. When they were cleaned, sewn, and covered with starch, so that not even a loose thread could be seen in the smallest grape of the beautiful bunches sprouting from a goblet, everything was ready. It was the moment to smother ourselves within the masses of worshippers, to become part of a world bigger than ours; four days of unbearable heat, of a happy and tragic holiday.

Thursday was a happy day because Jesus had invented communion, but Friday was a day of sorrow because he had been killed. That day we could not make any noise, we could not listen to the radio, only play in the yard some quiet game, like Tarzan. Andrés used to climb the mango tree and I could only follow him if I was Chita. If I wanted to be Jane I had to stay at the bottom of the tree, in the jungle house, cooking and taking care of Quique, who was Boy. Since I wanted to climb so badly, most times I exchanged my human identity for that of a monkey.

On Holy Saturday everything was returning to a normal level again, and on Easter Sunday we were dressed very elegantly for mass, and afterwards the entire family arrived for lunch. In the small garden next to the driveway, my aunts would release two or three white rabbits and hide candies and eggs. When we were very small we truly believed it was the Easter bunny who brought them. The world was perfectly ordered and unchangeable, but something new had arrived in our world, and it was Uncle Sergio, who suggested we bury Daruel *in absentia*.

My uncle did not speak much but he would talk with us in the afternoons when we returned from school. As he got to know us and realized that after two weeks of Daruel's disappearance we still missed him very much, he told us that the most logical thing was to make a funeral in his absence — *in absentia* — as he told us it is said in Latin. "If you convince yourselves that he won't return, that he's dead and buried, you won't be worried anymore, and if he returns, it'll be a surprise. Either way you'll feel better."

"But he'll never forgive me if I forget him," I answered.

"You never forget, but you learn not to let it hurt so

much everyday. Everything gets better, you'll see. Everything hurts less, right María?"

"I tell them all the time not to be morbid," added Mami instantly, as she loved to give mini-speeches about feeling sad or being a cry-baby. "In this country everyone loves to be a martyr, nag, nag, it's always the same thing, crying, suffering; you must learn to forget sad things, to leave the past behind, to be strong and not make a mountain out of a mole hill for every little thing. I had Laddie Boy and he died when he was seventeen, remember? That beautiful dog who used go for a dip in the ocean behind the Presbiteriano Hospital every morning. And he died because it was God's will, and what can't be cured must be endured."

"Well, it's true," continued Uncle Sergio after Mami's sermon, "sadness calls for measures. Let's have a memorial party for Daruel. We'll bury him symbolically, and then we'll take a deep breath."

At sunset, as we sat in the living room and absorbed the sunlight filtering through the jalousies and illuminating the greens and blues of the oil paintings of Capri and Mallorca which filled the walls, Andrés and I tried to be polite and understand this uncle who was taking his time to invent for us a ritual of death. He took pencil and paper and began to take notes.

"You've told me he was a good cat, right?"

"Yes," we answered in a chorus.

"Who were closest to him?"

"Lidia, Quique, Micaela and I," said Andrés.

"Then the four of you must attend. What was the deceased's favorite time of the day?"

"Around four, when he became more playful and

we would throw him a spool of red thread that Mamá gave to us."

"So it'll be at four. Let's bury him near the place he slept. That way he'll feel better . . ."

And he went on like that for a while. We had buried other animals before: a little duck of mine, some of Andrés' fishes, and one of Mamá Sara's geese which, according to Micaela, died from fright. Also when I was a few months old, they buried Negri, a mutt that looked like a mastiff "with sharp canine teeth and a golden heart" according to Cousin Germánico. It was Mamá Sara's favorite dog and Andrés took pride in saying that he remembered her because he was present when they buried her. He told me that he watched when they buried her under the house, in that enormous basement of fragrant earth, but he didn't remember the exact place, and sometimes obsessed with not having seen Negri, I would hide and dig throughout the basement with a shovel searching for Negri's grave, to find her, to be able to say, "I also saw her," even if by then she was only bones. For that reason I liked Uncle's suggestion of burying Daruel in the yard so he would not be trapped in that dark basement.

That evening, following Uncle's instructions, I asked Mami to bake cat-shaped cookies for the reception after the funeral.

"OK. Mami? OK? Will you make 'em?"

"Will you make *them*?" Mami corrected me.

"Well, will you make them? Yes?"

"For Sergio's plan?"

"Yes. It's nothing morbid, honest. It's for a snack after the burial."

"Don't bother Mari A. with your nonsense," interpolated Sara F., who was sewing.

"It's none of your business; you aren't my mother," I told her adamantly.

"Don't be disrespectful," Mami whispered in her special tone and I lowered my guard.

"We'll have to send this child to an institution," Sara F. began to nag. She enjoyed criticizing us as much as she liked taking us on outings. "Stand up straight; don't bend over; close your mouth when you chew; look at Germánico's daughters, they act like little English girls whereas you . . ." She was elegant, skinny; she smoked stylishly, and she knew the capitals of all the countries and of all the states of the United States by heart. Sometimes I thought she meddled in our affairs just to annoy us, and then I would answer back, because one must defend oneself. I was always defending myself.

That night Mami signaled with her head for me to leave, meaning that everything was all right, and she said: "Yes I'll bake the cookies. You tell me which day you need them and the night before I'll make them."

I was leaving the living room when I heard Uncle saying names in French. "Gauguin, Braque, Renoir, Degas."

"What are you two doing?"

"Playing," said Andrés.

"Playing what?"

"Uncle is guessing who painted the pictures in the calendar." Andrés was turning the pages of Aunt Ele's calendar of Famous French Paintings, and from across the room Uncle could tell who had painted them!

Andrés turned to a picture of a room, all in red, with furniture that didn't look finished, Uncle Sergio said "Matisse," almost without thinking. "Matisse," he repeated. "It's spelled M-A-T-I-S-S-E but the last letter isn't pronounced." He knew all the artists.

"How do you know them?"

"By the style."

"But how, how? What style?"

"After you've seen many paintings by the same artist, you learn a painter's style, his way of painting. Then when you see another painting by the same artist, even for the first time, you know it's his. The same thing happens with music or short stories; for example, if you read Sherlock Holmes stories, you know Conan Doyle's style."

"I read Sherlock Holmes stories."

"That's what I mean. You know his style; it's not difficult."

"But when did you learn about painting?"

"At the university, and afterwards on my own, by reading and going to museums."

"We'll also go to the university," I said, hoping to become just as smart. I picked up the calendar and looked for the painting by an artist called Matisse. "What else did he paint?" I asked.

"Do you want to see?"

"Yes, yes, yes!" we screamed, showing off. Uncle went to his room and brought out a folder full of pictures and clippings from magazines. He showed us many of Matisse's paintings. He was a Fauvist, he explained, a group of painters considered "savage," who used lots of bright colors in a unique way.

"That's why Lidia likes him so much, because she's wild," Andrés began to tease.

"And which one do you like?" Uncle asked.

Andrés searched among the clippings and took

out the Mona Lisa. "This one, I like the Mona Lisa. Aunt Ele will take me to Europe when I turn fifteen, and I'll see the Mona Lisa."

"He likes her because she's chubby, and he likes plump girls," I said in revenge, and right then he pinched me hard on my arm, and I signaled with my left hand, "I'll get you later."

After that day, Uncle Sergio decided to teach us what he called "something about art." We always insisted on French painters because Aunt Ele swore that France was the most civilized country in the world, and we should aspire to be like the French. Cousin Germánico was the only one who disagreed with her. "I wish I'd been baptized 'Británico' instead of 'Germánico'," he lamented. He adored everything British, and he argued that it was impossible to speak about civilization without the Magna Carta, Shakespeare and Winston Churchill. Uncle Sergio never said that you had to be from one country in particular to be civilized; he only showed us paintings and taught us how to study and appreciate works of art.

"Isn't it true that the French are the best painters?" I asked.

"No, there're good painters everywhere. Picasso, the most famous living painter, is Spanish, and there were marvelous Italian painters during the Renaissance, and there have also been excellent British and American painters."

"But no Puerto Ricans," I said.

"It's true," Andrés agreed. "There are no famous Puerto Rican artists because Puerto Rico doesn't have much culture and this island is too small. Only now as part of the U.S., as a Commonwealth, has

Puerto Rico begun to progress. If we are Americans then paintings by Americans are ours, right?"

"Art is a universal patrimony; all art belongs to everyone, but every nation has different forms of art," answered Uncle.

"Well, I don't care if there are or aren't good painters in other countries, I like the Fauvists and that's it. And I like Matisse's paintings," I said.

"I didn't think about it before, but it's natural for you to like Matisse."

"Why?"

"Because many in our family like him; it's inherited," he pointed out. Unlike the rest of the Solises, Uncle Sergio was not very talkative, and he would say things like that without explaining them further.

The funeral was two days later.

As we dug into the earth strange insects started to appear; long, white snails thin and sharp as pins, and little waxed pebbles, ignored cemeteries of minuscule creatures that were so familiar to us. When we were small kids, Andrés and I dug a lot in the earth looking at all those snails in which, invisible to the human eye, lived the parasites that appeared in Nati's films. Now we dug again and felt the earth so close. For a moment, we forgot we were digging a grave as we grabbed the tiny shells from the earth, looked at their geometrical forms, and felt linked to them by the smell of earth and the humus covering our fingers. Then returned to the present and continued digging with a gardener's trowel until we had a little grave two feet deep.

As soon as we finished digging we lowered a coffin

into the grave, a cardboard box painted with flowers and cat scenes and covered with an old kitchen towel that we had taken from Mamá's closet without permission. Inside was Daruel's invisible corpse. After we covered him with soil, I placed blue flowers on his grave, and Andrés opened an edition of the New Testament. As we had seen many times in movies about pioneers and seamen, he began to read a random passage:

"The next day, as they were on their journey and coming near the city, Peter went up on the housetop to pray, about the sixth hour. And he became hungry and desired something to eat; but while they were preparing it, he fell into a trance and saw the heaven opened, and something descending, like a great sheet, let down by four corners upon the earth. In it were all kind of animals and reptiles and birds of the air. And there came a voice to him, 'Rise, Peter; kill and eat.' But Peter said, 'No, Lord; for I have never eaten anything that is common or unclean.' And the voice came to him again a second time, 'What God has cleansed, you must not call common.'"

And then he closed the book. Uncle Sergio, Micaela, Quique, Andrés and I quietly walked back to the house leaving Daruel's corpse behind.

Thus, one afternoon, in the time before Fidel Castro became the embodiment of evil, and when you had to fast the previous night to receive communion, Andrés and I learned how to bury Daruel, in absentia, in the front yard of our house where he used to nap.

After the funeral procession entered the house we went to the back veranda where Uncle Sergio had arranged a snack for the mourners, as he called us.

On a table used to butcher chickens he had placed a linen tablecloth, colored napkins, wine glasses and sweet Spanish wine. There were meat pies, mints and the cat-shaped cookies Mami had baked for us. Uncle Sergio had us eat and toast to the disappeared, as he referred to Daruel, and he allowed each of us to drink two glasses of wine. Then he started to tell us how some savages eat the flesh of chiefs from other tribes and missionaries in order to acquire their strength and knowledge. He told us that it was highly symbolic and a very ancient ritual for us to eat the cat cookies so we would absorb all our love for Daruel.

The afternoon was coming to an end, the sky was painted with the colors of the Lenten season and, certain that we would have Daruel inside of us forever, our pain receded. Afterwards Uncle Sergio remained quiet as he examined the veranda: the large oak closet where the big pots were kept, enormous pots to boil *pasteles* for Christmas, pans to fry *tostones* for thirty people, the sink where Mamá washed freshly killed chickens, and the wooden trellis which faced the backyard where now dusk was settling over the pigeon house, and pensively he said, "The light here is truly special. It colors everything in a different way. In New York, dusk isn't like this. It's pretty but nothing like this."

"There's no country prettier than Puerto Rico," exclaimed Aunt Ele, drifting into the kitchen like a zeppelin. She always said the same thing. "Neither the green of Ireland, nor even the green of Switzerland, the most impressive country in the world, can be compared to the green here. In Santurce we have beautiful light because we're between two bodies of water: the sea on one side and the harbor on the other. Although, I'll tell you something, the Mediterranean Sea is . . .," and although no one wanted to listen to her, she'd carry on like that, happily offering comparisons of the world's geographical beauties, including that of our notable island, where progress was now arriving, as Uncle Roberto used to say and Andrés repeated, thanks to Muñoz Marín. But Nati believed the opposite.

"Shameless villain. Scoundrel!"

When we went into the living room Nati was again fighting with the governor. Every time he appeared on television she screamed at him.

"Papá said it: they're all Communists!" she would exclaim.

Papá was my grandfather Fernando. He had said many things that Nati, Mami, Aunt Ele and Sara F. repeated often, but I never heard him say any of them because he died the day before I was born. I always imagined him as austere and severe, as upright and stern. I used to feel ashamed because I was certain he would not have liked me — me with my bad manners and my hunchback from not standing straight. His death had pained my family so much that they probably cried more over his death than celebrated my birth, but, at that time, my arrival was the only thing that brought some happiness to my family. I have pictures to prove it. They show five women all dressed in black. One of the women is holding a chubby baby dressed in white with a bow on her head. That's me in the midst of my family in mourning for Papá.

Papá had foretold, among other things, that

Muñoz — since he had been pro-independence and a Communist in his youth — was going "to bring independence through the backdoor," and Andrés and I, as kids, feared that something evil called independence was going to arrive through the veranda door on any night when we least expected it.

Muñoz's face appeared on television while the news reporter explained that soon a new dam would be inaugurated, generating an extraordinary amount of the electric power needed to bring more industrial progress to our Island. But Nati continued to denounce Muñoz until Mami asked her to be quiet. "Shhhh, wait. Something happened in Africa." Something terrible had happened; some Africans had killed some Europeans. They had chopped them into tiny pieces with their machetes.

"That's terrible!" Nati screamed.

"They're the Mau Mau," informed Sara F. who read the most magazines and newspapers.

"It's the Communists' fault," said Nati. "They go there to plant hatred between whites and Negroes."

"Who are the Mau Mau?" asked Mami.

"It's a secret society that kills whites," interpolated Andrés, and I supported him.

"It's true Mami. We saw a movie about the Mau Mau."

"You see? I tell you it's the Communists who want to destroy the world." Nati spoke agitatedly.

"Why?" I asked.

"Because they are the anti-Christ; it's in the Bible; it's the evil that comes before the final judgment when the world will come to an end!"

"The world is going to end?" Andrés and I asked at the same time.

"Don't say that to the kids; it scares them." said Mami.

"Don't worry, it won't end soon," explained Sara F., "but the Communists and the Masons are the anti-Christ. They don't respect anything, people or democracies; they want to bring down the Pope in Rome and put a temple dedicated to the Devil in his place."

"The Communists?"

"No, the Masons my child. It's in the new book Monsignor lent us."

"Here they come," said Mamá Sara.

"Who?"

"*The Untouchables*," she said thrilled, since what my grandmother liked most was the federal government and all programs about the F.B.I. and similar organizations.

"But we'll never be able to carry on a conversation like this!" exclaimed Aunt Ele.

"Why is it that in this country we all have to talk at the same time? Why can't we speak about one topic and then go on to another? And why do we speak when the TV is on?"

It's true that we all liked to talk at the same time; it seemed so logical. We turned on the television and we all began speaking at the same time, five different, intertwined conversations, and in the middle of all this commotion some of us were asking for silence so we could listen to the TV; the entire family, there together, notwithstanding the warning of Pope Pius XII, which my family often repeated.

At first Mamá Sara had objected to buying a television set, so a few years went by before a TV was allowed in my house. Andrés and I listened to the

Three Villalobos and Tarzan's adventures on radio, but by that time everyone else in the neighborhood had a television and you could see small antennas beginning to appear on top of houses in Santurce. The first kid to have a TV on our street was Hamilton Martínez, Dr. Martínez's son, and by the time they bought us one, he already had a special screen to watch color television. It was a plastic screen, with three horizontal stripes, one blue, one red and one green, that was placed in front of the TV so you could see pictures in three colors. Aunt Ele said it was a silly thing, that surely the Germans would soon invent a true color television, and she did not buy us a plastic screen, but we longed for one throughout childhood.

In order to get the TV, we promised to say the rosary every evening right after dinner. We devised a way of saying it in record time so we could watch the programs we liked, which began at seven. Eventually she began to get interested in adventure programs like *Gunsmoke* and *The Untouchables* and shows about the police, so we were left on our own to recite the rosary and it was relegated to later in the evening.

"Pius XII said it: 'Television is both a blessing and a curse,'" Sara F. repeated like an oracle as she sat down to watch TV and opened a bag of candies.

"Why?" asked Andrés.

We always asked "why." Sometimes we had the impression that adults left thoughts unfinished precisely to get us to ask why, so that they could make speeches. That was how they tried to indoctrinate us with a mixture of scientific and religious concepts, true and false, liberal and conservative, products of their fears and prejudices, their wisdom and beliefs —

information which took us a lifetime to reorganize and debunk.

It was implicit in Life itself that there was Good and Evil and whether it was admitted openly or in passing, we knew that every action, every individual and every idea was judged by our family according to this standard of Good and Evil.

On the good side were the Catholic, Apostolic and Roman Religion, the Pope, the United States, the Americans, Eisenhower, Europe, especially all the refined Europeans, Grace Kelly, white people, all the militaries, Franco, Evita Perón, opera, *zarzuelas*, everything Spanish, including mantillas, sausages and the singer, Sarita Montiel, and absolutely everything German and Swiss, from Rhine wines to cuckoo clocks.

On the evil side were the Communists, atheists, Protestants, Nazis, newly formed black African nations (because in the process they spilled European blood and killed nuns), Puerto Rican Nationalists and any Puerto Ricans in favor of independence, mambo, Trujillo, Batista, and the Mexican actress, María Felix, the wicked woman responsible for Jorge Negrete being in hell.

"When he was about to die," explained Sara F., as if she had been there, "the priest came to him and said: 'Do you abjure that woman?' and he answered no, so he didn't receive absolution and he went straight to hell when he died, because he had lived with her out of wedlock."

That's why we could not see her movies, not even on television; it was unforgivable to be a bad woman. "Do you go to hell if you live with someone who is not your husband?" These were the clues about being an adult that intrigued us.

"No, not if you live in the same house, like in a guest house or a hotel. Only if you live together like when Mamá puts the doves in a cage together."

"But she marries them," we answered.

When Mamá Sara caught a pair of doves and put them together in a small cage or a box she always said "I'm marrying them." She was like a priestess, she had that power. Priests were the only ones with that power on land and sea captains at sea, but in our yard Mamá Sara had that authority.

"Well anyway, it's the fault of the woman," concluded Sara F. "Women who misbehave are evil; they do it out of viciousness. On the other hand, men, often can't avoid it; men have a wolf inside . . ."

Sara F. did not continue because we heard steps on the balcony and Monsita and Quique singing together: "In Spain people don't bathe; in Japan they don't because they have no soap; in Korea they don't because of the war; in Puerto Rico they don't because of the Constitution."

"It's not like that," I said when I opened the door.

"And in England it's because of the coronation."

"Oh no."

"Oh yes."

"Don't say that about Spaniards," said Mamá Sara from the hall. She never wanted to hear anything bad about Spaniards because Papá was from Spain.

"Go play somewhere," ordered Uncle Roberto when he came in. We knew that meant that they were going to speak about things that were none of our business. After the visitors gave a kiss to each adult in the household, Andrés, Quique, Germán, Robertito, Monsi, and I went out to the backyard.

My family was always happy to see each other, and even if they just left for the morning, when they returned in the afternoon they kissed again. Uncle Roberto arrived with Aunt Clara to plan an outing to celebrate the opening of the new dam. He was going to escort an executive who was coming from the United States with his wife and kids. We would have to go in several cars.

We went out to the yard and down into the basement under the living room, we moved a bench and took turns standing on it with an ear stuck to the living room floor, and that was how we learned everything that was none of our business.

"I already spoke with Germánico. That's why I stopped there and took Monsita for a ride. That girl is always so pale; they should take her to the beach more often."

"Well, let's get to the point," said Aunt Ele who was always so practical.

"O.K., we have my car, yours and Germánico's, but I think we need one more because . . ."

At that point Andrés got bored and came down from the bench to speak with us. Then, without being on the bench, we heard Nati exclaim, "How terrible!" We ran to climb back on the bench. Andrés got there first, but they were speaking so loudly that just by climbing on boxes all of us could hear.

"How awful. Such a handsome kid," said Nati.

"Yes, my dear, queer. That kid turned out queer on poor Tati Almeyda. Yes, she sent him to the United States, far away to California. That's where people say they're all sent. But Dr. Reollo was on the same plane. You know that his passion is San Francisco and the Grand Canyon, and everytime he can he goes there on vacation," explained Aunt Clara.

"My dear, he even does his eyebrows."

"How sad!" said Mami.

"What do you mean, sad? He just needs to be put in his place. Give him to me in the National Guard for a few weeks, and I'll kick his butt until I straighten him out!" exclaimed a convinced Uncle Roberto.

"You can't cure him. At his age it doesn't change."

"That's why boys need a man when they are growing up. That faggot was always with women . . ."

"You see, you must be careful," said Uncle Roberto. "Andrés should be allowed to hang out in the street more, to become a man, and not be always surrounded by women."

"Just a moment. You leave Andrés out of this. He's a little man through and through." Mami leapt to his defense. Mami never allowed anyone to say bad things about us.

"Listen to that, a little man," said Germán in the basement darkness.

"Don't be a pain; don't tease Andrés," I intervened.

"They're afraid you'll turn out queer," he said to Andrés.

I clammed up awaiting the ensuing fight, but Andrés answered in a mocking tone. "You're the queer because you're Hamilton's friend."

"And what does that have to do with this?"

"Hamilton was caught by Pedro and Gago trying to take off the pants of the Santiago kids. They were building a garage at the doctor's house, and he was hiding with the kids behind the house. Pedro told the doctor, and Micaela and Aunt Ele.

"What's it really mean to be queer?" I dared asked, although I was supposed to know.

I am convinced that Andrés and Germán measured me with their eyes to convince themselves that I was old enough to know and Andrés said, "Come here."

Immediately we all went over to them. "No, not all of you. Quique, Monsi and Robertito must stay behind because you're small."

We big kids went out to the yard. Andrés answered me: "It's when a man acts like a woman, likes perfumes and flowers, puts on dresses instead of pants, and has manicures and all that."

"I know that, but what does trying to take off the kids's pants have to do with it?"

"To give it to them in the back."

"To give them what?" Andrés and Germán looked at each other and neither wanted to say what we assumed we all understood. You were always on the verge of knowing the truth, but everything always remained half-truths.

"Forget it," said Andrés.

And all of a sudden Quique shouted, "Margara is going to have a baby," and we all ran.

"Get down," Andrés ordered, and he repeated what was being said upstairs.

"No one knows who the father is."

"Since she's always hanging out . . ."

"It must be one of those bums who visits her father."

"Her father is not a bum," Uncle Sergio said, followed by a brief silence, since he never spoke or argued.

"No, not him. But some of the people who visit him are . . ." said Mami.

Margara's father was a Nationalist but not like

those who never bathed. At that time there were some very dirty, homeless men who had beards and long sticky hair. Their faces, their torn clothing, their arms and their legs were all the same dirty color. Every time we asked who they were Nati would say they were crazy Nationalists who had sworn not to cut their hair or take a bath until Puerto Rico was free. But Don Gabriel was not like that. He was a sweet old man with blue eyes and a lot of white hair; he was very clean and quiet. His house was just behind ours, but the enormous wall that divided the houses on our street from those on his did not allow us to see his house. We saw him sometimes when we walked on his street returning from the beach on the other side of the San Gerónimo Fortress. He was always on the porch talking with other old men.

"Remember Margara grew up without a mother, but she isn't the only one in that condition. From her it was expected, but I bet you don't know who else is pregnant? The Puerto's second girl, the blonde one."

"No!"

"Yes!"

"That kid is only seventeen!"

"How awful!" said Nati.

"Yes, it seems her boyfriend ate the cake before the wedding."

"But the rumor is that it wasn't the boyfriend," Aunt Clara said severely.

And we all waited for the revelation.

"The rumor is that it was the uncle, the one who went to the war!"

"Jesus!" said Mami, "how repugnant!"

"They'll have to send her to Spain, to study, of course, so she has the baby there. That's what people say, that it was the uncle. That's why the boyfriend doesn't want to marry her because otherwise, there would be no problem."

"What's happening in the world!"

"It's the Anti-Christ!" sighed Nati.

"The world has always been this way," clarified Uncle Roberto.

"Oh no, now everything is worse," said Sara F. "Look at all the robberies and even assaults. A month ago, there were robberies in Monchita's and the Flores's backyards. They took all the good clothing that was hanging out to dry. And three days ago they robbed Alejandro's small market near Bus Stop Twenty. Two robberies in less than a month! That never happened before."

"People are talking about putting iron bars on their houses and in some places have already done it."

"Oh no, no way. That would take away all the charm from this house; I'll demolish it before I put iron bars on it," exclaimed Aunt Ele who was always painting and fixing our house, and planting trees and flowers so it would look pretty.

Almost all the houses in our street were two or three storey wooden structures with overhanging roofs, decorative towers and gables, and all the houses, from the Roja's, the smallest, to the Soto Morales', almost a mansion, had names inscribed at the bottom of the entrance gate or on small plaques embedded in the walls facing the street: Villa Mercedes, Villa Sol, Villa Margarita. Ours was Villa Aurora, the House of the Dawn.

Sara F. always told the story and we loved to hear it of how Papá, Fernando Solís, one day had suddenly bought Villa Aurora and returned to Mayagüez with the surprise that they were moving.

"We were still very young. Sergio was not yet born, and Papá Fernando decided to move because another doctor had found him an office in Old San Juan in the Padín Building facing the Plaza de Armas, and it was necessary for us to move to San Juan. First he thought we would live in Old San Juan, in the family's house on Luna Street, but there was a dispute over that house with some cousins and relatives who had surfaced all of a sudden, and turned out to be members of our family.

"Uncle Bartolomé had the wolf inside," explained Aunt Nati "and those so-called sons kept the house. So we couldn't move to the family house in Old San Juan, but what a good thing that turned out to be, because that area is disgusting now and we loved this house the moment we saw it."

"Papá was always right. He thought everything out so carefully. He was a brilliant, impeccable man," continued Sara F.

And in pictures he looked just like that, always dressed in a three-piece linen suit with a Panama hat and a pine cane. He had arrived in Puerto Rico in 1896 to work as a doctor with a maternal uncle, who in letter after letter to Mallorca told him how wonderful the climate was. "My grandfather left 'for a few years' and never again saw his fatherland," Sara F. would say in her most dramatic tone. "Then he met Mamá."

"Isn't it true she was French?" Andrés asked.

"No, no. Her mother was from the French islands, her father was Canarian, from the Canary Islands, Manuel Villegas y Castro, and her mother was Marie Dubois. When Mamá was three years old, her mother died. And at seventeen she was already married to Papá. From Marie Dubois you inherited your green eyes — both of you, your father, may he rest in peace, and Sergio . . ."

Among Mamá Sara's grandchildren, the Solís' green was the exclusive patrimony of Andrés and me, and, although it was not mentioned often since in my family all kids were praised equally, we knew it set us apart. We were orphans — a forbidden word in my house — with pretty green eyes inherited from a mysterious French lady from a faraway island. In Papá's studio, converted into a study room for us and a sewing room for Sara F. and Mamá Sara, there was a faded photograph of the famous great-grandmother looking out at the world with a serious face and very clear eyes.

We sat there in the afternoons to do our homework, and now, often, Uncle Sergio sat next to us to read or to search the shelves and bookstands that lined the room, and amongst Papá's old books and papers, for all the things without any value which families value most: faded photos from family trips, birthday cards, old eyeglasses, everything that had been left behind in the corners of the study for forty years.

In the afternoons the sun fell on that side of the house, and the heat enveloped us in drowsiness. Mamá didn't allow anyone to speak to us while we were studying; it was like a convent with its vow of silence. Mamá, who never went beyond the fourth grade, but had the prettiest handwriting in the family, taught all of us to read and write; she was convinced that learning required utmost discipline, and that only through reading in complete silence, without even looking to one side, could wisdom become eternally inscribed, as if by some kind of intellectual magic, on the minds of the Solís.

Andrés, Quique and I communicated using tiny notes that we rolled on pencils and passed from one to another when we didn't want to do our homework or had already finished it. Mamá Sara didn't think it was possible to study for less than an hour and a half or two hours every afternoon, and at 2:30 she'd sit in the study to sew and mend, and in complete silence, we were forced to work.

When Uncle came in she'd smile at him and put her index finger in front of her lips, like the nurses on the signs for "Silence" in a hospital, but with a smiling face, as if she were the satisfied guardian of our academic future, content in her protective role, a grandmother hen looking at her little chicks in a small rural school, while we dreamed of flying the coop.

One day Uncle Sergio saw a message I was passing to Andrés. He took my pencil, unwrapped the tiny piece of paper, and read: "When tarmangani comes in, I go out for sopu," and smiled at us inquisitively. It was a message written with words from the Ape language. For many years Tarzan comics came with an Ape-Spanish dictionary which we memorized, and the three of us used to communicate secretively. Our plan was that when Uncle, the tarmangani or white man, came into the study I would take advantage of that moment to go to get some food, sopu, crackers or something like that, which I would hide and take back for the three of us.

Uncle observed the rules, and when Mamá got up to prepare our snack, an unequivocal sign that the study period had ended, he asked us questions about school and whether we liked to study, but not like those other adults asked. He began by telling us that all his life he had hated the little bow that all students had to wear around their necks up until the sixth grade in Christ the Redeemer School, which we were now attending and he had graduated from.

"I also hate it," said Andrés.

"What I hate is the wine color of the uniform," said Quique.

"And I hate that they won't let us wear moccasins and we have to wear those awful tie shoes," I said. "It's not like that in the United States, is it Uncle? I've seen in magazines that girls wear moccasins."

"Well, in some schools yes. I don't know about parochial schools."

"I don't like history or grammar," explained Andrés.

"I don't like math or grammar," I said.

Quique didn't complain about any subjects, only about religion because he was afraid of sister Claire.

"She scares you because she's very strict," I explained.

"But I've heard your mother say that your school isn't that strict."

"Not like others, right Andrés? We do our homework in two seconds and we all have A's. Our school is not difficult."

"And do you want to change?"

"Mami has said that maybe they'll move us to another one but I don't know."

"And why do you write strange words in your messages?" he said, taking out the Ape-Spanish note. He caught us by surprise.

"If you want, we'll teach you," Andrés said as he took out his copy of the Ape-Spanish dictionary. Uncle took it with him and promised to memorize it in a week. "It's easier if you read the comics, because when you see the drawings you associate them with the words," explained Andrés who was the smartest of the Solises. Uncle smiled along with us and afterwards we even considered making him an honorary Apache.

The following Sunday, after going to an early mass, we ate breakfast quickly and waited for Uncle Roberto to arrive for the outing. We were dressed in our Sunday best, inside and out, since it was important to always have clean underwear, so that what happened to Conchita Salazar would not happen to us. "One day she fainted in the middle of Ashford Avenue. They took her to Presbiteriano Hospital, and when she awoke on the stretcher, sobbing, she begged your Aunt Sara F., 'Sarita, for God's sake, take off my girdle. Don't let the doctor see this dirty, old girdle that I put on because I was just going out for a moment.'" Aunt Ele would often tell us this story and urged us never to wear underwear that was showing its age.

Before we left we had all also gone to the bathroom, so we would not have to go in an unhygienic place and be marked for life just like poor Stinky Charito. "She was my classmate and one day in the third grade," Mami narrated solemnly, "she farted when she bent over to pick up a piece of paper and ever since we have called her Stinky Charito. That continued throughout high school and after she entered and graduated from the university. Even now no one remembers her real name; she remains

Stinky Charito. That's why you must move your bowels before leaving the house so you will not become a subject of ridicule."

Every Sunday, duly fearful of the embarrassment that we could suffer in the outside world, we dutifully readied ourselves with clean outer and inner clothing and purged intestines for Mass and the family outing that followed.

That day Uncle Roberto borrowed a station wagon large enough for ten people, and between it and our enormous Oldsmobile and Cousin Germánico's Studebaker, dressed in our Sunday best, we all went to the grand opening of the dam to listen to Muñoz's speech about the progress it would bring.

When we arrived there were hundreds of people walking along a muddy path through the grass, a shortcut leading directly to the dam. Instead, we walked along the river bank, and all the time they screamed at us: "Give me your hand. Don't get too close to the edge. Don't get dirty. Don't get sweaty."

And Aunt Ele added, "Be nice to your little friends." The little friends were the children of the executive Uncle Roberto was escorting. A girl my age and two smaller kids. They all wore sandals and did not have on their Sunday best.

Their father, Mr. Arnold Killey, was Puerto Rican. When the visit to the dam was over and we had dropped them at their hotel, Sara F. immediately began to criticize them. "Look at him, a hick like that representing the government of the United States." He had changed his real name, José Arnaldo Quiles, to succeed in the States. Uncle Roberto called him "Arnie" and after that they became best friends for many years. His wife was an American, and that was precisely what my family objected to the most.

"Did you see how untidy those kids were? And she's so dull, with that awful perfume. That's the problem when a Puerto Rican marries an American; they make an awful couple."

"You heard it Andrés," I said to him. "Don't ever think about marrying an American."

"Don't bother him," Mami jumped in.

"Yes, leave him alone," said Aunt Ele. "What we're trying to explain is that in any group of people there's always one, the men or the women, who work harder. In the case of Puerto Ricans, the men are lazier; for Americans, the women are very lazy."

"Yes, that's the way it is," continued Mami, "and they're very untidy. They don't take care of themselves, they don't iron their husbands's handkerchiefs, they never iron, they buy their children wash and wear clothing so they don't have to iron. You can imagine, when two lazy ones get married their children suffer."

It didn't seem to us that Barbara and her little brothers suffered much. Their parents let them jump in the mud and get dirty, and they told us they didn't have to wear socks or shoes in the house. But my family knew best, and that's how we learned that marriage between a Puerto Rican man and an American woman was not a good thing, although the reverse was O.K.

"Also American women use cheap perfumes that are made there and sold door-to-door," added Sara F. "Americans are very good people, but they're not sophisticated; they don't know about French perfumes or European crystal. Good God!, they have such provincial taste." As simply as that she opened and closed another chapter on world culture.

But even if they lacked refinement, Americans had to be admired and loved more than any other people, because they were good. They had saved the world from the Nazis, and now they were protecting it from the Communists. Also they were geniuses when it came to technology and progress. The dam we had just visited had been designed by Americans along with a few Puerto Ricans who studied in the United States. Mami also praised them constantly.

"May God bless the American who invented the washing machine!" she yelled one Saturday from the yard. Andrés smiled and peeked through the banisters of the staircase. I looked too. When Mami saw us she went on with her praise. "Yes, because you don't know how it used to be; we had to wash so many things by hand that our hands were cut and sore from scraping the washboard," and she started to sing as she put clothing through the wringer piece by piece.

Mami only sang religious songs she had learned when she belonged to a church chorus in Juncos, and a few passages from *zarzuelas*, Spanish operettas, that stuck with her when she saw them performed at the Tapia Theater. She washed clothes to the tune "Christ has died, Christ has risen, Christ will come again." She pounded meat as she sang "Saint Catalina was the daughter of a kiiiing, the daughter of a kiiiing; her father was pagan but her mother was noooot." And she made the beds singing "Lord, have mercy. Lord, have mercy. Christ, have mercy. Lord, we have sinned against you. Lord, have mercy." Usually we accompanied her, but that day as she wrung out clothing to the tune "Let's drink, let's drink wine, because it makes us forget love's pains," we didn't feel like doing anything. We had awakened, just like the Puerto Rican men and American women, feeling a terrible laziness which lingered in us and kept us in low spirits.

Mamá Sara was the first to notice: "A storm is coming," she said when she went out to feed the doves.

Micaela agreed with her. "Yes, it's true we'll have bad weather."

"Oh Mamá, it can't be. The people from the weather bureau haven't said a word," said Nati, as she had breakfast in the veranda.

"Yes, a storm is coming. The animals are all very quiet, the canaries won't eat, the chickens are still, and even those two kids are quiet and listless," said Micaela.

Mami left the washing machine for a moment and looked around. "It's true," she emphasized. "Look at the light, how strange it is. It's a day of a rare brightness, copper-colored; it's not normal and it smells like rain, but there are no clouds in the sky."

We began to feel the silence and to look at the strange colors. There was a very peculiar calm. Not even the neighbor's restless dogs were barking. When we were sure that these were unequivocal signs of a catastrophe, Andrés and I ran through the house warning everyone: "Aunt Ele, wake up, a storm is coming; Uncle Sergio a storm! Sara F., a hurricane is coming!"

At eleven a.m. the radio announced that a storm was approaching. Aunt Clara called to say that all of us had to go to her house, since it was a big, cement house, and it had a bomb shelter in the basement.

But no one could convince us to leave our house.

"Although it's made of wood, it will hold," said Mamá, "but we must board it up."

We mobilized immediately. Andrés and I were indescribably happy. It was so exciting to break our routine, to wait for what we thought would be an adventure like in the movies, to become heroes, to save people on the verge of being swept away by the storm, and to survive, because at that age one believes that one will survive, move ahead, never die. Uncle Sergio went to the basement with Andrés and Nati to get boards, nails and tools. We had to shut the windows and cover the many glass windows and seal the holes in the dove and chicken houses. Mamá Sara and I immediately made a shopping list. Mamá Sará insisted on buying a case of twelve cans of Spanish olive oil.

"But Mamá, we already have at least five cases!" said Aunt Ele, but Mamá insisted. Ever since she could not get olive oil during the Second World War she had been obsessed with it; we always had enough oil to last us several months in the pantry under the staircase. Mamá was getting old so we had to humor her. Uncle Sergio winked at Mami, and when we were heading towards the door he showed up with a case of oil from the pantry.

"Let's put this in the trunk. That way Mamá won't feel bad because we didn't buy it."

We were about to leave when he stopped and looked pensive. At the entrance to the house Aunt Ele was lighting a candle to the statue of the Virgin of Mount Carmel.

"The lares," said Uncle Sergio.

And he repeated, "Yes, of course, the lares, and

inside . . .," and he walked to the semi-circular arch where, behind a glass door, were the pictures of Papá Fernando, our great-grandmother from Mallorca, Papi, and some other relatives.

Aunt Ele turned on her heels. "What did you say, Sergio?"

"The lares and the penates, Elena, don't you realize? Just as the Romans, just as in Pompeii." Aunt Ele lifted her head trying to remember.

"The Romans," said Uncle Sergio "put images of the lares, the gods that protected their houses, at the entrance to their homes, and inside were the busts of their dead ancestors, so that they would be protected, just like we do."

"No, we do it like they did," corrected Aunt Ele, "and you're right, because also in Herculano . . ."

"Herculito," said Mami interrupting the exchange. "You can talk about that later; let's go, everything will be bought before we get there. People will empty the markets today!"

At four o'clock in the afternoon everything was ready. The animals had been given food for a few days. "Just in case we can't go out to feed them!" said Mami, who remembered San Ciprián and San Ciriaco hurricanes and was terrified of storms. The oil lamps were full of kerosene, and Andrés had taken out all the National Guard expedition equipment Uncle Roberto had given us. Each of us was wearing hiking clothing, heavy boots and a vest, and had strapped around us an army belt from which hung a canteen, electric flashlight, small first aid kit, army rations in dark green cans, and a metal helmet. Piled in a corner of our informal dining room were military capes, shovels and picks, bullet shells, and a pair of blue, training hand grenades with red safety locks. Sara F. was always afraid of them; she swore that, by mistake, one of those grenades could be live and Andrés and I used to tease her. "One . . . two . . . three . . . BOOOOM," we'd scream.

"Get them out of here; grenades aren't needed in a hurricane," said Mami. "Get the map." Andrés put it away every year perfectly folded. It was a very old map of the entire Caribbean. On it were marked all the hurricanes that had hit Puerto Rico since we could read and write. It stunk like a dead cockroach, but it was a family treasure. We turned on the radio and we put another battery-operated one nearby in case the electricity failed. Aunt Ele filled the bathtub and many pots and pans with water in case the water supply stopped. While we waited for the news from McDowell, the American weather forecaster, my family talked to us about the horror of storms.

"During the Saint Ciriaco hurricane a page from a newspaper got imbedded in the trunk of a tree in Río Piedras."

"During Saint Ciprián the roof of our house in Juncos flew off, the rain came in, the side panels and doors of our armoires cracked, and we lost everything."

These stories managed to scare us a little.

"Could the roof of this house fly off?"

"No, dear me, it's well secured."

"But could it fly off? It's made of galvanized zinc."

"Well, it could happen; but it won't."

"And all our things could get ruined?"

"Bring them down here."

We ran to our rooms on the second floor to select our most important belongings. I wanted life to be like this forever, exciting, unreal, without a routine, with no need to worry about which clothes are proper to wear at home or outside, without them always telling us to stand straight. The approaching tragedy had broken all the rules, shattered the order, you could be whatever you felt like. I took a pillowcase and began throwing in my favorite comics.

"Only fifty, choose only the best fifty," said Andrés.

"Why?"

"You can't take them all, only fifty," he insisted, and I listened. We had hundreds and each of us had our favorites. Andrés also had foreign coins, and I had many letter openers and a metal box that had a lock and had once contained nougat where I kept my private things, my bracelet and favorite earrings. I also had a Japanese doll that my father had brought back from the Second World War and my mother said was worth a lot. Now I kept it hidden and safe, just in case I decided to leave home someday. I would sell it and manage to survive.

We went downstairs and we wrapped the pillowcases in pieces of old, plastic bathroom curtains. We sealed them with tape and tied them with rope.

"Now, what're you going to do with them?" asked Sara F.

"The best thing is to bury them so they'll be safe," said Mami. As a form of entertainment, she often sent us to dig holes in the yard, since she hardly ever permitted us to go out to play with other kids in the neighborhood. I was not allowed because there were no other girls, and Andrés couldn't go because he would acquire bad habits from the neighborhood boys his age who didn't come from educated families. They kept us occupied in the house as much as possible and hole digging took an entire Saturday.

We asked Uncle, because he was one of us, if he wanted to protect something special. He smiled and said no, but soon afterwards he called us and handed us a plastic bag containing several books, a few small, sealed cigar boxes and a compass. I was moved because he entrusted his most important possessions to us. Andrés looked at the compass, "This compass is broken Uncle; it only points south."

"Yes, I know. It's a memento."

"Who is it from?" I dared asked, feeling the right to do so.

"It was a present from cousin Andrés," he said.

"Papá's cousin, the one who disappeared?"

"Yes, from him."

The three of us went out to the yard. I didn't ask any other questions that day, but I felt peculiar knowing something about Andrés, our strange cousin, such a close relative and so mysterious. His photo was on Mamá Sara's dressing table and Papá had mentioned him in his will. He had only visited the house two or three times, but everyone remembered him as the most handsome man in our family. In his honor my father was named Gustavo Andrés, my brother Andrés, and my cousin Germán Andrés. He had touched my family very deeply and was always spared from their accusations about how opportunistic most of our relatives were.

"Relatives are like old rags; you only need a few and you should keep them far away from you," Aunt Ele quoted Papá Fernando. But Mami said that it was not so because we continued to be close to so many cousins and uncles and second cousins, on Mamá Sara's side of the family, who lived all over the island.

I carried Uncle Sergio's belongings, and as we were about to go down to the basement and bury our things, Uncle saw that the wind had bent some branches of the loquat tree behind our house onto the electric wires. "Those branches should be cut," he said. "Andrés please get the ladder while I look for the machete. Lidia, there are still some things scattered in the yard. Please pick up those boards and cans. If a strong wind comes they'll fly around and kill someone."

We immediately started to work. Andrés brought the ladder and we put it up next to the tree. Uncle climbed up and began to cut the branches. After a while he looked over to the other side of the wall, at the yards of the houses that backed onto ours: the house of the Villamils, the house of the spiritists, and the house of Don Gabriel Tristani, Margara's house.

Then we saw him look, think for a moment, and finally call out, "Don Gabriel, do you need help?"

Don Gabriel said hello to him. "What a surprise! Sergio, my boy, how are you? I heard you had arrived, but we have not seen your face around here."

"Wait, I'll come over."

Uncle jumped onto the wall, pulled up the ladder, threw it over the wall and disappeared. Andrés and I dropped everything and ran after him. We looked for the small ladder and used it to climb the loquat tree in order to watch Uncle as he dared go to Margara's house, and even worse the house of that Nationalist, of a NATIONALIST! When we were able to balance ourselves, we saw Don Gabriel and Uncle Sergio embracing and Margara extending her hand to him.

"Bring us coffee my child, go ahead," said Don Gabriel.

"Don't you have any sons here to help you?" asked Uncle Sergio.

"No, my boy, no. The oldest moved inland, the other four are in New York, my oldest daughter and her husband are in Hawaii with the army. You already know that. Now I only have Margara, who's pregnant."

"Well, don't worry; I'll help you," said Uncle, and he began to nail some large boards over the windows of their small house.

"My boy, it's only going to rain," said the old man.

"You don't think the storm will hit us?"

"No, you'll see. I grew up in the countryside and I can tell that it's near but it won't get us."

But Uncle Sergio went on nailing boards. The house was small and yellow, had a minuscule garden all planted in pigeon peas, and also had two or three fighting roosters in their cages. On a pole next to the house, waved a faded, tattered Puerto Rican flag.

"Come down here right now. What's going on?"

Mami caught us *in fraganti* as she used to say.

"It's Uncle Sergio . . ."

But she didn't let us finish.

"It's nothing. What Sergio does or doesn't do is none of your business. He's a man and men don't need children following them around and interfering in their lives. I've told you this a million times!"

Of course he's a man, I thought. If he weren't, he wouldn't dare go where he just went. I was a woman; I could not visit that house of evil people, of Margara, of the Nationalist. We returned home and it seemed like an eternity before he returned. Mami began to cook. "We believe in one God, the Father, the Almighty, maker of heaven and earth, of all that is seen and unseen. We believe in one Lord, Jesus Christ, the only Son of God . . ."

"Mami, come here," screamed Andrés.

". . . by the power of the Holy Spirit He was born,' I can't now. I'll come in a little while."

"Mamá Sara is calling you."

". . . of the Virgin Mary, and became man . . ."

Mami continued in the kitchen. She was waiting for the hard-boiled eggs to cook, and she timed them with Creeds and Lord's Prayers. Just then Uncle Sergio returned through the kitchen door.

"Was the old man all alone?" Mami asked him.

I noticed how she said "all alone." I heard it clearly, and although I didn't fully realize it at that moment, inside of me I felt something I had never before noticed in Mami, clemency, a very brief and clear gesture of tolerance and compassion towards those people; although, in thinking about it, I realized she had never spoken badly about Don Gabriel or Margara. It was Aunt Ele and Sara F. who berated them.

"Yes, well no. Margarita was there, but he didn't have anyone to help him board up the house and that's why I went."

Mami took a deep breath. Aunt Ele came into the kitchen and went directly to Uncle Sergio: "You didn't have to go there; don't look for trouble. Why did you have to go?

And immediately she reprimanded me. "Lidia, get out of here."

"Come, let's go, " Mami said.

"I'm not a dog," I answered, "I'm not a dog; I'm not Fido, 'Leave, Lidia, out of here'."

"Do me a favor and stop the tantrum," Mami yelled

at me.

I left. I obeyed grudgingly and felt like screaming. I'd miss all the drama that was certain to take place in the kitchen.

Mami took me to the other side of the house, to the informal dining room.

"Sit down," she said. "You must learn to control your temper, do you understand? In that respect you are like your father. In a man it's tolerable, but in a woman it only leads to vulgarity and arrogance. You must learn to control yourself. If you get angry, you'll only end up getting angrier and angrier because your body secretes a substance called adrenalin. You have to pray so God gives you the humility to control yourself and not be insolent, do you understand?"

Mami spoke softly. She always used to give this same speech when I had tantrums as a kid, and now she was repeating it. "But I want to know why he . . ." but she didn't let me finish.

"It's natural that you find all this confusing. I'll explain what you should know and nothing else. The Tristani were always very respected by your grandfather. He and Don Gabriel always greeted each other. Although Papá didn't agree with Don Gabriel's politics, he always respected him. The children from his first marriage are all serious and hard-working people. The sons fought in Korea, the daughter is married to a soldier. But this Margara, from the second wife, grew up wild. Her mother was a vicious woman and the daughter turned out the same."

"But why did Aunt Ele say to Uncle that he . . . "

"That's all you need to know for now. Your aunt only wants the best for us. It's not good to visit the Nationalists. In the 1950 uprising they wanted the government to fall. You shouldn't mingle with people like that because people will believe you are like them. If they need Christian charity, you help them, but you should never mingle with them, or say hello to Margara when she walks by the front of our house.

She knew it! She knew it all. As always she knew it all!

I went to the second floor. Sara F. was spellbound looking at the sea through her window. "I bet it looks better from the tower," she said.

At that moment Uncle Sergio came up. "Yes, let's go to the tower; I haven't been there in years."

I had never gone; Andrés and Germán had already been there a year before. You needed long legs to get there.

Micaela joined us. "Let's go to the tower." The adventure continued.

"For God's sake, be careful," screamed Aunt Ele and Nati. We reached the attic by walking through Aunt Ele's big back room, and then, through a wooden door, we entered a place where the beams came together, the entrails of the house; it was like being in Villa Aurora's skeleton. There were many spider webs, ants, and termites, and small albino roaches because the sunlight never came in there.

Sara F. was carrying a lantern, and we had two more. We walked on boards laid across the joists, at the end of which we had to stretch, hover in the air, and jump across a large gap to the next board. The gap was almost a yard long, and there was a drop of many feet. After crossing, we were on a small platform, and we entered into a cupola with its glass window. Aunt Ele opened the window. In the distance the sea seemed swollen with rain. "It must be very rough underneath even though the surface looks so calm," said Aunt Ele. The rest of us did not say a word; we stayed there for a while looking at the sunset. The air we breathed was the freshest to have entered that space for many years.

The storm never arrived although we all expected it to. The house easily withstood the rain, wind, and the simulacrum of a storm. The sun came out again in two days. In other parts of the island many trees had fallen down, in the south all of the harvest was lost, but Santurce went almost untouched.

"It's the Virgin of Mount Carmel that protected us," explained Mamá Sara. In our house everything returned to normal, but having held Uncle Sergio's most treasured possessions in my hands only enticed me to find out more about him, about his things, about the secrets men keep, since we long ago had learned women's secrets by heart.

Uncle Sergio had received two boxes of books by mail, but besides that he barely had any personal belongings. We usually sneaked into the closets of the adult members of the family after our afternoon snack, when Mamá and Micaela were preparing dinner, and the others had not returned from work. I would station Andrés on the staircase to stand guard, and Quique would patrol the porch in case someone arrived unexpectedly, while, with old keys, pins and tweezers I opened armoires, small chests, jewelry boxes, and locked drawers in wardrobes, and then I'd call the lookouts to snoop around with me in these private belongings.

Our fingerprints were all over the metal chocolate boxes with views of Switzerland on their lids in which Mamá Sara kept her things. In them she kept hundreds of dimes — the only things she ever collected — a pair of worn bifocals, a gold cigarette box, the small black silk boots our great-grandmother wore on her wedding day in Mallorca, and letters, written in faded brown ink on stationery with the letterhead of the Spanish Society of Mutual Assistance and Beneficence, which always began "My dear Sara" and ended "Your beloved Fernando." Usually they were about patients and medicines and belonged to the period of time when Papá worked at the Auxilio Mutuo Hospital in Río Piedras. There were also recriminatory letters from Papá Fernando's mother complaining because he never returned to visit. There were medals awarded in expositions in France and Spain for the agricultural products of the farm that once belonged to our family, prayer books and novenas, and a photograph, from the time the regent princess and heir to the Spanish throne visited the island, cut from a newspaper and mounted on cardboard. These were grandma's secrets. They smelled of talc and old age.

Mami kept pictures of all of us and none were hidden. There was one of her as a kid with the two aunts that brought her up after her parents died. And one of my father, in front of the university tower, and another of him dressed as an army captain. She also had our report cards and all the birthday and Mother's Day cards we had given her. Just like Mamá Sara, she kept everything unlocked, probably because she kept her true secrets safely hidden in her memory.

Aunt Ele had two or three small coffers and jewelry boxes, some contained miniatures from her collection, others held dolls from another collection and many photos. She also had small poetry books in which she dried and pressed wildflowers. Later on she would take them out to make souvenirs and bookmarks with embroidered edges. She had an ornate Spanish cabinet with a secret compartment behind a drawer, which she had ordered from Europe. We searched that compartment anew every few months with great anticipation to see if there was anything important, but we found only papers, canceled bank books and passports, some curls identified "Andrés," "Clara María," "Sara F.," and "Quique," and tiny pieces from broken pins and earrings that someday she planned to get fixed.

Sara F. had the most secrets, but we never discovered what she considered valuable. In an empty almond box she kept her collection of sapphire jewelry, two pairs of earrings, one necklace, three rings, one brooch. In a locked box in the bottom drawer of her dresser she had soaps, perfumes, pencils, lighters, boxes of matches, band aids and old pills. Her bedroom was in such disarray that in the same drawer she had nightgowns, boxes of Kleenex, bags of candy, papers, newspaper clippings, and light bulbs. We opened and closed everything taking utmost precaution to leave all the contents in place. This was very difficult with Sara F.'s belongings.

Nati kept the three-door armoire in her bedroom locked, and only once was I able to open one of its doors. It was where she kept her shoes and her best clothing, each pair of shoes placed in its own box, every dress ironed to perfection. We were never able to find any of her other secrets.

Uncle Sergio, on the other hand, sometimes left his closet door open. In it he had his broken compass, his small, sealed, impossible to open cigar boxes, a box of watercolors, a pipe he never used, leather bookmarks, and his books, all of which he had annotated.

Andrés, Quique and I were not only getting accustomed to him, but we were becoming a part of his life. He memorized the Ape-Spanish dictionary and sometimes used it to send us short notes. Occasionally he accompanied Mamá and us when we walked on the beach on the other side of the San Gerónimo Fort, and after returning home, before it was time for television, he played parcheesi with us or chess with Andrés. Slowly he convinced Mamá to free us after a half-hour of homework so he could teach us art history, and she agreed, although I don't think she understood what that involved. Then he took out some army manuals about European art, some art books and books of paintings, and, from encyclopedias, he had us copy prehistoric hieroglyphs, Roman architecture, Egyptian hieroglyphics and Mayan steles, and he began to awaken in us a visual sense that we hadn't known existed.

"This is the true sixth sense," he said. "Besides observing, you can sense pleasure through your eyes if the light, color, and the texture you see are in harmony. For instance, when you look at the different shades of green in the garden or the tiny white feathers on the breasts of the carrier pigeons, what you feel when you see such variation is visual pleasure." He taught us to look at, to sense, the backs of small lizards and their infinite color combinations; to recognize by its brush stroke if a picture was Oriental, European or Pre-Colombian; and he told us to choose the work of art we liked best so he could order big prints for our rooms for Christmas. Without hesitation I chose a Matisse still life, Andrés a Botticelli virgin, and Quique the mysterious Iberian Lady of Elche, which he stared at dazedly in the encyclopedia, and, when he thought no one was looking, would kiss on the lips.

But some days Uncle Sergio woke up like a deaf-mute, and we understood that on those days he wouldn't speak to us at all; he had a deep and all consuming sadness. He left his room only a few times, to go to the bathroom and to eat, but the rest of the day he spent locked in his room, and we heard him sighing and pacing back and forth. Sometimes he went out to the grocery store across the street to buy a beer, and returned to his room which smelled of the stale smoke of smoldering cigarette butts.

At these moments I longed more than ever to be with him, to share his secrets, and to understand what was happening. My intuition told me it was something important and passionate; I wanted to be a part of it, but he never allowed me to.

Sometimes, after his periods of sadness, he tried to talk to us about things other than art. One day Nati took us for a walk, and we passed a school named Segundo Ruiz Belvis. Andrés asked who he was and Nati said, "Oh, I don't know. One of those shitheads. Who knows? A politician. Sort of a national hero. You know here everyone is a sacred cow after their death."

Uncle waited for her to finish and almost whispered. "He was a very important man in our history."

"What did you say?"

"That he was a very important man in our history, an abolitionist. He helped the cause of justice in

Puerto Rico. He was against oppression . . ." and all of a sudden he became silent. Nati was looking at him impassively. It seemed to us that something bad had happened.

"Well, Sergio already explained it," she said, and we continued walking. Years later, when we questioned them, my family denied ever having requested Uncle Sergio not to speak to us about Puerto Rican history, but we believe they did, because he never spoke to us again about any eminent Puerto Ricans and we never again asked him about them.

"I wish you could have seen from up close how pretty she was. She's the only woman I've ever seen with peach-color skin; even her tiny facial hairs were peach! It was during my first trip to Spain. At eight o'clock in the evening, when it was still daylight in Madrid, I was watching from a window facing the square as a lavish parade began to move towards Cibeles Square. First came the King's halberdiers wearing period costumes, then Franco's Moorish Guard mounted on white and brown horses and wearing matching uniforms, and even the horse's hooves were polished and painted. Then Franco and all the government elite. And finally she appeared, beautiful, in a gorgeous bright blue gown, with matching coat. The ignoramuses from *Life* magazine criticized her for not knowing how to dress. Can you imagine? Back then the flight from Argentina to Spain took twenty-eight hours, and it was very cold in the planes! Planes weren't acclimatized like today. She had gone directly from the plane to the reception on the square, so of course she didn't have time to change . . .

"And we met again in Granada. One morning I

went to see the cathedral, and when I was there who arrived but she, and I was as close to her as you are to me, like this, we were three feet apart, in that enormous cathedral, and she was so pretty, the most beautiful woman I've ever seen; there we were just me, my guide, Evita Perón and her entourage . . ."

Aunt Ele would tell us anecdotes from her trips anytime we complained about school. It was her way of motivating us to study so we would graduate, go on to the university, become professionals, and be able to travel, since you never knew when you would be part of an historical moment like that.

"I'll travel to Australia," said Quique," to see kangaroos."

"I'll go to Egypt to see the pyramids," Andrés pointed out.

"I'll travel to Rome to see the Coliseum and to Perú to see Machu Pichu."

"Isn't it true that she shouldn't go to Latin America, Auntie?" asked Quique.

"Well, just to see Machu Pichu, the pyramids in México and the Pan de Azúcar in Brazil, yes, but not to wander around like you can do in European cities. It's a very sad region. Only poor, hungry, very dirty Indians live there. Argentina is worth visiting because people there are like Europeans, but the rest of the continent is very sad, and you don't travel to get depressed but to amuse yourself," she would explain and proceed to change the subject.

"But in order to travel, as you already know, you must be cultivated, you must speak other languages, and above all, you must learn to eat many different foods. You can't be provincial about food."

She said this for the sake of Andrés and me

because we refused to try new dishes. Quique was like the rest of the family: he didn't have to be begged to try new foods. At the slightest invitation, he would gobble down anything.

"You will remain hicks as long as Mari A. pampers you with beef steaks and French fries," came Sara F.'s voice from the kitchen. "Come here. Look. I bet you don't know what this is," and she showed us a root of an indescribable color.

"I don't know, and I don't care," I said.

"Stop the tantrum! See? She'll have to go to reform school," she screamed, just to annoy me.

"It's a *yautía*," said Quique.

"That's it. You see, he knows."

"And this one?"

Silence from the three of us.

"A *lerén*."

"I don't care," I repeated. "That's the food country bumpkins like. Why do you tell us that we have to eat everything to be sophisticated and then try to get us to eat the junk that hicks eat? I like to eat fried steaks and French fries, and Andrés likes mashed potatoes. That's what he'll get to eat in the army when he goes. And I eat hot dogs, and he eats hamburgers, and I eat grilled cheese sandwiches and drink Cokes. I'll never like those soups, root stews, and the other junk you make."

"Idiot, *lerenes* are not eaten in a stew," she said in a mocking tone.

"You're the idiot," I screamed at her and left.

I wanted to be sophisticated so they would take me traveling, but although I tried, I couldn't be. Something was happening to me, but I didn't know what. I felt like crying every time they told me I was not cultured, when they predicted that the French, who were the most refined people in the world, would not like me.

"No Frenchman will kiss your hand because you bite your nails; look how ugly they look. If the eyes of a person mirror the soul, the hands reflect refinement. Unmanicured hands portray a person who does not wash herself, who is untidy by nature. You'll have problems if you continue like that," snorted Nati, while she filed her long nails on Saturday mornings. She would call me over so she could file and manicure mine, but she never found anything to file.

"This girl won't turn out well," complained Sara F., restarting the fight.

"Don't worry, she'll learn, won't you, Lidia?" said Mami, coming to my rescue.

"Yes," I'd grumble and leave with her for the market.

On the way Mami would say hello to lots of people and I had to greet them too, which bothered me a lot because each of them would have something to say about me and I hated them all. That morning everyone had some comment.

"Look how big she is," one of the Castros said.

"She's almost a young lady," Mrs. Rojas notified us point blank.

"Be very careful to whom you give your little heart," Monsignor Serrano said, which seemed to me the most stupid and ridiculous thing anyone could say and only made me feel like a sinner because deep down inside I was angry at one of God's representatives on earth.

We went to church so that Mami could speak with Augusta. She was a tiny black woman from the islands. She was almost a hundred years old and dressed like a doll in a long, white satin dress taken in at the waist and a white, wide-brimmed hat. Her life centered around helping the deacon arrange flowers and replace the burned out candles with new ones. Mami was one of the few people who understood her English, a jargon sprinkled with a few French-sounding words which spilled out through her two remaining teeth.

"Cabring yeloflo tdei," she said.

"She says: 'I brought yellow flowers today,'"

Mami translated and went on talking to her for a while as I insisted, "Let's go. Let's go, O.K., Mami? Mami, I want to leave."

"Don't be a pain; let me speak to Augusta."

"But I'm bored."

"So what? Wait and don't bother me."

After a while we left for the market. In front of the Fomento Bank Mami always bent over to give a few cents to a greasy-haired man in a filthy jacket who spent his weekends there, surrounded by bags full of old newspapers. He rarely spoke to anyone, but he always spoke to Mami.

"Good-bye Pepe," she said to him.

"Good-bye and thank you, María Angélica," he answered.

"Poor Pepe and his sisters," Mami always began. Pepe Gauthier was a lawyer who went crazy. "He was brilliant, from a good family, an extremely handsome, white man, and one day he returned home and went crazy. Since then he has roamed the streets with those bags full of newspapers. He doesn't eat, he drinks a little, he reads and reads, and he crawls along the street. How his sisters suffer!"

"OK, but let's go."

"You must learn to be more sociable," Mami said to me. "You can't be like that. You should greet people and speak to them."

"But what can I say to an old black lady I don't even understand or to vendors at the market who don't know anything about anything or to that beggar?"

My mother didn't reply but remained pensive. After a while she said as if thinking aloud, "God willing, eventually both of you will change."

Yes, we were changing and constantly becoming more introspective. Half of the blame was theirs because they were so overprotective that we were unsociable towards anyone who was not part of our immediate family. Television deserved the other half of the blame because it showed movies in English every afternoon which kept us apart from the rest of the world. Mamá Sara loved to watch them, and since she didn't understand English, the three of us spent our afternoons watching television and translating for her. After a while Uncle Sergio joined us.

"Pope Pius XII said it clearly: 'Television is addictive,'" Nati repeated constantly when she returned home from work and found the television-watching quintet eating soda crackers smeared with butter.

On Columbus Day they showed a movie about Columbus. It was the same one they had year after year on October 12. In school, we had to do a project about Columbus, individually or in groups. That year, Andrés and I had won second prize. After looking closely at the details on nougat boxes, which always had representations of Columbus arriving in America, I drew and colored the discovery scene and

Andrés wrote a poem that he later copied onto silk paper using green ink. Our project was awarded only second prize because Dr. Martínez bought a book in New York about the conquest of America for his son, Hamilton, from which Hamilton cut more than thirty colored pictures, pasted them on white cardboard, added text typed by the doctor's secretary, and then had Pedro the Stutterer build a folding screen to hold the exposition.

"Of course he won because of his father's money," said Mami.

"No way, that had nothing to do with it. The boy selected everything by himself," answered Sara F.

"But money always has something to do with it," said Mami.

"Please María A., that boy must amuse himself with something now that he has only one parent."

When Andrés heard this he glanced at me and took advantage of the moment to bring up a subject that was never mentioned. "We don't have a father either," he said.

"Ah, but that's something else," Aunt Ele answered immediately.

"You have never lacked anything, and you never felt the pain of losing your father; you were very young. Poor Jefferson, I mean Hamilton, lost his mother only two years ago. Two years! And his mother. That's not the same."

"Why not?" I asked.

"Because only mothers who bring you into the world know how to give the special love that children need. What I mean is that fathers love their children a lot, but they aren't the ones who bring them up. They can't take care of them like a mother."

We ended Columbus Day by thanking God because Columbus discovered us and brought Catholicism and the Spanish language, and because we had a mother, which was something that Hamilton, even with all his money, no longer had.

"Just think! Columbus was a saint; he was going to be canonized," Mami explained to us as she tucked us into bed after our prayers, "but he committed one rebellious act against God. When he returned to Spain, they were about to remove the chains some scoundrels had unjustly put on him, but he didn't let them because he became arrogant and haughty, and that single act cost him his sainthood."

"You mean he's in hell?"

"No, no, but he couldn't be canonized because there was proof of his rancor, and a spiteful person can never be a saint. It's a terrible sin." I knew that the entire speech was aimed at me, but I played dumb and went to sleep.

Months before Christmas we had already gone through the Sears catalogue, but this year we felt strange. When you realize you're no longer a child, and you see all those toys that no longer interest you, you still daydream, imagine and long for them. That's why I asked for a Davy Crockett hat, a globe, and a set of oil paints. Andrés asked for a model of the aircraft carrier Saratoga, new swim fins, and a globe which was smaller than mine but had the continents in relief, a detail we would fight over on Christmas Day.

A few days before Christmas Eve we went to Catalán & Sons to buy all the things my family considered delicious, but which I would not eat under any circumstance: nougat, almonds, hazelnuts, highly-seasoned pork sausage, marzipan, candied fruits, nuts, dates (which I would never eat because they looked like roaches), figs (which I would never eat because I was sure they tasted like roaches), along with jams, salamis and sweet wines, (which Andrés, Quique and I drank secretly).

On December 23, Eloísa and Baltazara, two elderly black women who had brought up my family, arrived at Villa Aurora. Mamá ordered us to put two tables in the backyard and, to my great relief, that noon they slaughtered the two piglets Mamá had — they would never again bite anyone. So we ate fresh roasted pig meat with its crisp skin, pork rinds, and blood sausage. We made *pasteles* of plantain and *yautía* filled with pork and beef, but mine had to be "blind," without any filling, otherwise I wouldn't eat them.

"This girl is such a pain," Aunt Sara would say, but Mamá Sara didn't pay any attention to her and tied small red ribbons to the plantain leaf wrappings of half-a-dozen *pasteles* so we would know those were for me.

On Christmas Day, after opening our presents, those of us who had not gone to midnight mass would go to mass at 10:00 in the morning, and from there we would go to old San Juan to see the Little Shepherd's Parade. That year Angelita and Monsi, Cousin Germánico's daughters, took part in the parade; it was their turn. All of us at some point had been little shepherds and had marched in the parade singing "Rejoice. Rejoice. Mary and her husband to Bethlehem go," as we rushed elbow-to-elbow through San Francisco Street. When we arrived at the Town Hall the mayor, Doña Fela, would be waiting for us. She'd give us candy and make a fuss over each of us.

Smelling fragantly, white-powdered, her lips and cheeks red like the Popular Democratic Party flag, her elaborate, enormous white streaked chignon interlaced with braids and flowers, she was the most Christmas-like woman you could ever imagine, Santa Claus' wife, if he had ever gotten married, as Aunt Ele would say. She was tall and beautiful. If only she hadn't belonged to the Popular Democratic Party, which placed her on our family black list.

On New Year's Eve, so we could practice our good manners, they took us to different restaurants for aperitifs, dinner and dessert, and when we returned home we tied dozens of firecrackers to the fence to wait for a midnight full of noise, light and joy.

The next day they gave us a surprise: they informed us that we had been recruited to work. They were going to pay us a salary and each one of us would have a savings account from which we would be able to withdraw money. I immediately went to practice my signature so that it would not be ugly when I signed my passbook. Quique wanted to know which color his passbook would be, and Andrés asked how much interest the bank paid. None of us asked about our jobs. It turned out to be fun sometimes, boring most times, and probably a scheme to get us out of the house in the afternoons to see if we could learn to mingle with people and be more sociable .

Nati, together with a Mr. León, who according to Mami, turned out to be just that — a lion — had opened a medical laboratory a few months before in the same building in which Aunt Ele had her doctor's office. As time went on she worked less and less at Tropical Medicine and more in the lab, since, as Aunt

Ele used to say, the most important thing in the world is to be your own boss, not to work for a salary, but to be the boss.

Mr. León eventually retired from the business and Nati became her own boss. The laboratory's location in the heart of Santurce, near hospitals and government buildings, was ideal, and soon they began to have lots of clients. They recruited us three afternoons a week to take care of small details: to wash pipettes, to organize all the small jars and strange glass tools, to clean the small tubes in the centrifuges, to stamp in purple ink papers, envelopes and pieces of cardboard with the seal of the Machado Laboratory, to make cotton balls, to boil needles and syringes, to place test tubes in their right place, and above all, to water the ferns and kill all the snails in all the plants on the balcony, in the waiting room, the room where they measured blood pressure and in the garden they had constructed on the small roof of the apartment that had become the laboratory.

We were not allowed to take the elevator alone because we could be abducted, although we didn't understand where to, so all day long we went up and down from Aunt Ele's office to the lab using the stairs. One day I went up one floor above the lab to the roof where a boy a little older than me was singing. His name was Manuel; he was very gentle and we became friends. In less than a month when we discovered that our favorite song was a forbidden merengue, "I placed my hand in a dark place," we became even closer, and although we didn't officially call ourselves boyfriend and girlfriend, we were certain that when we grew up we would get married.

Both his grandmother and mine had forbidden us to listen to merengues, but we never understood why. "I placed my hand in a dark place" was the most melodious and catchy song we had heard. Manuel sang to me everyday and we planned that some day, after our marriage, the two of us would work. I would be an archeologist, and he wanted to be two things: a baseball player and a singer.

"You can't," I said sententiously. "You have to decide. You can't have two jobs. You can't go to a club to sing and have a baseball game that same night."

"Why not?"

"Because it can't be. Look at your mother. She has one job, the beauty parlor, and my mother is a secretary, Aunt Ele is a doctor, and Uncle Roberto does economic development."

"What's that?"

"Well the people from Fomento have a desk covered with papers and they work with those papers on that desk for a long time, and they often go to the airport to pick up Americans and they take them all over the island; that's what they do."

"But I'll do both jobs," he said and turned on the radio to WKVM — the favorite station of maids — and we called in secretly, using pseudonyms, to request that they dedicate a song to us.

When there was absolutely nothing else to do and the horrible heat began, the heat you feel in this country at about three o'clock in the afternoon, we would go onto the roof adjacent to our building and pick up hundreds of nails, pieces of wire and scraps of wood. There were always pieces of junk on all the roofs. Manuel said it was because workers were so happy when a building was finished that they never cleaned the top floor, which is the roof, so they left everything in disarray, and since the owners never went up there to check, the workers got away with it.

One day Manuel told me that his mother was going to move, so we decided to abandon our wedding plans because he had not yet decided what he wanted to do with his life, and I knew I was not going to stay in Puerto Rico. Many years later I found out that he was a chess genius, and that he had turned out, no-one knows how, to be pro-independence.

Nati was afraid of rats, found frogs repugnant, and felt sorry for guinea pigs since their entrails were so tiny they could not be observed accurately to make an exact diagnosis, so it was decided that in our laboratory the pregnancy test would be done with female rabbits. We all went in a three car caravan to a neighborhood in Juncos to buy two male rabbits, selected by Uncle Sergio, and four female rabbits, selected by Mamá Sara and Uncle Roberto. Pedro came and built some rabbit hutches along the backyard wall. Andrés and I would climb on top of them and hang from the branches of the breadfruit tree to try to look over at Margara's house, but we could hardly see anything. Uncle had never mentioned the Tristanis again, nor had anyone else in my family. But we knew that they still lived there because Margara walked past the front of our house with her big belly. They were forbidden to us, but we wanted to see them.

Soon we had to build another rabbit hutch in the yard to separate the males from the females because, as Nati explained to us scientifically, just the scent of the males caused the ovaries of the females to become inflamed, and if that happened the pregnancy tests could turn out wrong.

Since Nati only used each female rabbit for tests about three times, and afterwards Mamá Sara kept them for breeding, we began to have rabbits, and then more rabbits. Nati would take an old doctor's bag from Aunt Ele and throw a rabbit into it for the trip to the lab. So she was etched in our memory as a blend of scientist and magician, so skinny, with her long, curly, red hair, carrying a black leather bag with the head of a sweetly-smiling rabbit sticking out.

Mamá Sara took advantage of the hutch construction to redesign the backyard. She had the old chicken house demolished and in its place Pedro the Stutterer and his son, the Little Stutterer, as they were called, built an enormous cage for the doves and the chickens, almost the size of a small house. It was a huge U-shaped cage, twelve feet high, with a pitched, zinc roof. The lower part was reserved for the hens and above hung tens of small boxes which were cages for the doves. The lower walls were made of wood and the upper of chicken wire to provide ventilation and sunlight. It took almost one hour every day to feed, clean and care for so many birds and their cages.

"We have to join the agricultural co-op," suggested Uncle Roberto. "That way the food will cost less."

One Friday afternoon we all went and Mamá became a member. We bought four large metal cans, and we placed them under cover by the basement entrance. In one we kept the food for the rabbits; in the second, the cracked corn for the doves; in the third, corn kernels for the hens; and in the fourth, lime flakes which were mixed with corn for the hens to strengthen the shells of their eggs.

None of us remembered that Mamá Sara was very lucky at raffles and games of chance. But once in a blue moon when her cousins came to San Juan from the center of the island — the ends of the earth to us — they reminded us that when Mamá was young she always won first prize in raffles during festivals and patron feasts. They also said that she had been like an Amazon, that she could ride a horse like no one else and she liked to dance a lot. I couldn't understand how Mamá Sara could have gone horseback riding and dancing so often if she married so young, and I imagined that she had always been like when I met her: serious, working busily from morning to dusk, sweet to babies, snappy with kids, dressed, as she was, in half-mourning clothes until the day she died.

At the co-op convention in March, she won a radio, two geese and twenty pounds of Café Rico. At the party on the eve of Mother's Day she won first prize, one hundred chicks. She left that place showing all her teeth. I still don't know why she liked birds so much more than other animals.

"Papá said it," complained Nati. "'Flocks of birds in cages don't pay wages.' Look how much it costs to keep so many birds, so many canaries, so many chickens, doves and geese!"

The garage had to be made smaller so we could build a wall on the back to make enough room to place the recently purchased incubator, and they also had to install a new electric outlet. For a while it was a novelty for us to watch the yellow chicks all peeping at the same time growing under the warmth of the bulb and protected from the rats by a double layer of chicken wire. Then they became rather nice chickens. But soon the deception was complete: they became full grown hens that continually pecked and shit like the rest we had to care for everyday.

When they built the new hen house, Aunt Ele wanted to give Mamá Sara another surprise, so she had Pedro the Stutterer and the Little Stutterer build a small stone grotto behind the loquat tree, with gigantic shells incrusted in the stone entrance. Aunt Clara and Uncle Roberto bought a statue of the Virgin of Mount Carmel, and a few weeks later, with lemonade, meringues, and cakes, our family entertained the neighbors who came to the blessing of the image.

During all those months of construction, animals, and change, our family had been trying to separate us as much as possible from Uncle Sergio because of an incident that we never understood very well. One day at the beginning of February, Uncle Sergio received a letter which provoked a family gathering and conspiracy. It arrived, and immediately he left for his room to read it. He remained there all afternoon and he didn't come down for dinner. The next morning he awoke with his eyes red from crying. He had cried. CRIED! A grown man. Uncle, had cried! Andrés and I were surprised, but we didn't ask anything. They sent us to the yard to play, but from the basement we heard Mami and Aunt Ele trying to get something out of him. He wouldn't talk.

In the afternoon, when I went by the informal dining room, I saw Aunt Ele, Sara F. and Mami trying to glue together many tiny pieces of paper. It was Uncle's letter. They had taken his torn up letter out of the wastebasket and were gluing it back together to find out what had happened to Uncle. When they spotted me I started to run, but Mami called me back.

"Lidia Angélica, come here right now and don't make me say it again."

They swore me to silence, that I would never tell what I had seen, but I felt like a traitor. I was in Uncle's camp, not theirs, but since I had sworn to God, I had to remain silent. They told me to leave. I quickly turned at the veranda and went into the small ironing room, next to the dining room where they were plotting Uncle's salvation, and hid under the ironing table.

"You must st . . ay the . . .re. Now danger . . .ous to return."

"Here's another piece," said Aunt Ele. "Mercedes is well and Doña . . ." It's unreadable. "We don't know anything . . . Was hospitalized . . . must be hospital-ized . . . very bad . . . "The truth is that it can hardly be understood, but it's all awful news, what can I tell you? The only thing Puerto Ricans are good at is complaining."

That night we went to Cousin Germánico's house. They sent us to play in the room Cousin Germánico had built which contained something incredible, an air conditioner. There they slept without mosquito nets and outside noises could not be heard. All of us kids threw ourselves on our cousin's bed to watch television.

"That's how it's now in the States, kids," Germánico said to us. "You keep the television in a bedroom instead of in the living room, and watch it comfortably, lying down."

As soon as he left I went into the bathroom to hear them talking about Uncle. I knew they had come for that reason.

"We have to get him a job. Being idle doesn't help at all."

"But doing what? He didn't finish college."

"No, but he knows English very well. He could be a teacher."

"You know they won't allow him to be a teacher."

"The same for Government jobs. They'll never give him one, at least not at this time."

"I could get him something in a factory; there are many opening up."

"Or as a door-to-door salesman, what he did in New York. Now it's fashionable to sell encyclopedias and books like that ."

"I got it," Germánico exclaimed all of a sudden. "Why not plastic bags?"

"What?"

"Plastic bags. Soon everyone will use them. People won't be allowed to put garbage out on the street in metal cans anymore. The sanitation workers will only pick up garbage that is in closed plastic bags."

"Where did you hear that?"

"It's going to be like that from now on; it's for hygiene."

"But that's too expensive. Imagine! Spending money to throw out garbage. It's absurd; I won't accept that."

"That's the way it's done in American cities. It'll be like that here."

"Well, doing something, whatever. We must get him a job," interrupted Aunt Ele.

"Yes, and we must separate the kids from him a little more. It's not good for them to hang around with someone who's depressed and taciturn all the time."

"Yes, he doesn't set a good example for them. The other day I heard him say that he didn't have to go to church to be saved, that a person who prays at home obtains eternal salvation," Sara F. squealed on him.

"How awful!" added Nati.

"And sometimes I think he drinks a little too much."

"He gets drunk in front of the kids?"

"No, he hasn't reached that point, but he walks around looking slovenly, he doesn't shave, comes downstairs in a T-shirt..."

"In a T-shirt?"

"Yes, just like the vendors in the market. He doesn't take care of himself."

"That's why we should be more like the English, who during the war, even as prisoners, shaved and groomed themselves daily. It's the only way to keep your human dignity," said Germánico, who always took advantage of any chance to praise his idols.

"In the meantime, we must keep the kids occupied, take them out. The afternoons they don't work they stay with him watching television because their school barely gives them homework."

"Then it's decided. In August, if they are accepted, they'll transfer to Nuestra Señora de la Asunción because the nuns there require an I.Q. test," explained Mami.

"A what?"

"I.Q., intelligence quotient. If they aren't intelligent, they don't want them because they would slow down the group."

"What a good idea. That's great; you'll see, they'll get in."

"But until they change schools we must take them

out more. They're too old to be kept inside the house so much. They should mingle with kids their age."

That was the reason we continued our swimming and diving classes. They began to take us to the movies twice a week, to kid's dances at the Casa de España, and to the beach on Sundays. With all the power their money gave them, which Uncle lacked, they were able to mobilize us and keep us away from Uncle Sergio.

But the influence he had on us, his irreverence, his so called "vulgarity," his destiny which appeared so different from ours, his sad glances, his letters which were messengers of pain, and his scent, especially, I insist, his scent, kept him deeply rooted in the daily routine of our simple middle-class life. A greeting in the morning, a small amount of time spent together in the afternoon before we left for the movies, and brief encounters in the basement when we fetched food for the animals, became painful moments of complicity. Painful moments because they made us feel an almost sweet-pain.

Adults never suspect — or fail to imagine — the existence of close and powerful ties between children and forbidden people. But children, even the very young, sense and recognize themselves in a forbidden person, especially if it is in their nature to become one. Andrés and I would see Uncle walking quietly down the street, poking around old chests in the house, speaking in passing with Micaela, visiting the basement too often, looking intensely and silently at the homing pigeons, sitting pensively in front of the television without really watching, thinking about something else, napping on the drawing desk at the top of the stairs, staring out the windows, and whispering a song as he showered. We followed a few steps behind him, not knowing if he realized we were there, but knowing that if he did notice our presence he didn't care. He was party to our vocation of being his shadow, and what united us was rich, complex and good, as good as can be the love of those who don't have any alternative but to love each other because there is no one else. He said that the three of us were unique because we were the only ones in the family with green eyes, although I knew and resented that Micaela also had greenish eyes, even if hers were not the true Solís green.

But Aunt Ele went ahead with her plan, and now we had duties on Saturdays as well as on some afternoons. She increased our salary from twenty to thirty cents per day, for sweeping the leaves in front of the garage, for picking up the milk bottles the milkman left at the bottom of the staircase at the back of the house, and for gathering the eggs from the hens around two o'clock in the afternoon. With twenty cents we had enough money to buy one comic every day and we still had some money left. Our salary had been in jeopardy a few years before, when Sara F. returned from a sudden trip to Europe.

The family had sent her suddenly because the Pope had died. In three days they prepared her for the trip she was planning to take that summer. The funeral was to be in three days, and Aunt Ele, who wanted Sara F. to enjoy herself, said to her the afternoon the Pope died, "Why don't we move up your trip?"

They called the State Department, and in one afternoon her passport was updated. They took her to the best stores — Giusti, Padín, and Velasco — to buy new travel clothes, and most important, they had the camera cleaned, because the reason for the trip was to have Sara F. document for the family, for posterity, the funeral of a Pope of the only true Catholic Church.

Sara F. came back with fourteen rolls of film. In nighttime scenes you could see the Pope's coffin, in daylight you could see rising smoke from the deliberation of the cardinals at the Vatican, in bright sunlight, there were eight rolls of flowers, gardens, more flowers, Belgian flowers, French gardens, Spanish flowers, German gardens, public areas full of flowers in Italy, Italy seen through foregrounds of flowers, and in a superb roll, taken in chiaroscuro, the Generalísimo Francisco Franco escorted by his Moorish Guard. Of all the hyperbole we grew up with in my family, the most florid concerned Franco's Moorish Guard.

"They are splendid!"

"They'd rather die than allow someone to hurt him."

"They are fierce and loyal, as the devoted personal guards of a leader should be."

"Is Franco the president of Spain?" we asked.

"Yes and no. He isn't exactly the president. He's the leader, the Caudillo, the one who governs."

"Spain isn't a democracy?"

"Yes, of course it is. The problem is that the Communists wanted to control Spain, and Franco and the army had to save Spain. But what the Spaniards want is a monarchy, like the English, and when Franco dies they'll have a king again."

Up to that point they all agreed. They argued about the future king because the arguments of both

Bourbon and Carlist lineage still ran in our family. Seventy years after having left Spain, three generations later, my family intently discussed the legitimacy of the heirs to the Spanish throne.

But besides the marvels of the Moorish Guard, whose atrocities during the war we didn't learn about until we were adults, the most impressive aspect of Sara F.'s trip was her first-hand introduction to the German style of child rearing.

A visit to her friend Dr. Von Schulow, a German who had studied in Puerto Rico and whose kids were Sara F.'s godchildren, had given her the chance to see how German children kiss their father's HAND before going to bed! They kissed their father's HAND before going to bed and they asked for their father's blessing before leaving the house. That would not go well with us; Mami would never allow such an unhygienic custom. But there was also distressing bad news. "What? You give the kids twenty cents a day?" In Germany for cleaning the entire front lawn of the house, almost a mansion, the good Doctor gave little Franz the equivalent of three cents. THREE CENTS!

They tried to institute a regime of three cents but the leaves piled up by the garage, and the cats licked the warm bottles of milk we forgot to retrieve from the stairs, and we again had our twenty cents per day, and the miserable salaries of post-war Germany were never mentioned again.

By the time Uncle arrived to stay at our home our salary was adequate and now, to keep us away from him, they had increased it, but not enough to pay for extra movies, so without realizing it they had given us the means to acquire another forbidden item: books about sex.

Our knowledge of the sexual nature of human beings was limited to two or three poorly understood jokes about a man who called his penis the car and a mother who called her vagina the garage and a kid who yelled: "Mama, Mama, Papa is parking the car in the maid's garage."

As far as we had figured it out, sex was a state of mind or activity intimately tied to original sin and the wickedness of women and the filthy bodies of men. When Skippy, a petite American blonde dancer, arrived in Puerto Rico and she danced on television wearing only a cabaret entertainer's costume which showed her thighs, the world was coming to an end because "Sex is now on television," Sara F. screamed.

And even though some things were not directly linked with sex, our family considered them dirty by the mere fact that they were related to the masculine sex, for men were thought of as something naturally dirty. Andrés was very clean, but when he grew up, would he, too, be classified with the dirty ones? When Uncle Sergio arrived home, Nati had put a laundry basket in the bathroom just for him. Until then we all had just one enormous basket where we put our dirty clothes, and Micaela emptied it every two days.

"This hamper is for Uncle," explained Nati when she put it there.

"Why can't he use ours?"

"Because he is a man and his humors, his perspiration, are different," she said unwilling to explain any further.

"And how come Andrés uses the women's hamper?"

"It's not a women's hamper. It's a family hamper!

Andrés is a kid, but Uncle is a man."

"And when he grows up, will he have his clothes apart from ours?"

"Go and play, I'm very busy," she avoided us.

The first chance I had, I lifted the cover of his hamper and smelled and smelled trying to establish the difference between the odor of his dirty clothes and the intermingled aroma from the clothes in our family hamper, but the only thing I managed to do was to identify his scent distinctly and forever. I sniffed his clothes in secret, just as I secretly searched for Negri's bones, or climbed to the highest branches of the loquat tree to look at the Tristanis' house, because it was my ill fate that all the things I thought of and wanted to do the most were not proper, and, although they would have been dismissed as child's play in other families, in mine, I knew, they were clearly forbidden.

So, as I involuntarily entered puberty, more obvious in me than in Andrés because boys experience such changes more gradually, and we all of a sudden go "off," as I was told menstruation is called. I realized I needed information that under no circumstance would we get in that house and from that family. I think the adults were aware of our curiosity because a few weeks after my first period Mami went to the religious bookstore in San Juan and came back with two lengthy books printed on terrible paper, but bearing, thank God, the Imprimatur and Nihil Obstat of the Church, which guaranteed approval by the Church and prudish content. Mine was called *You Are Becoming a Woman* and Andrés' *Now That You Are a Man*. It immediately struck me that the title of my book didn't categorically establish and assign to me the same degree of adulthood that the title of Andrés's book did. I wanted to know how men were and Andrés wanted to know how women menstruated because Jenny Silver had been taken out of her classroom screaming in terrible pain, and all the boys thought it was her period, but they didn't know what was happening and no one would tell them.

That same night Mami gave us the books, after she made us both promise that we would not exchange them because they were "individual and private reading," we immediately traded the books and locked ourselves in our rooms to try to understand all those dirty and evil things that came about because of sex, all of humanity's suffering, all the pain in childbirth God had given to women for tempting Adam, all the responsibility that accompanied the divine grace of holy matrimony, the sanctity and honor of the priesthood (although if God didn't choose you for that vocation, marriage was second best), the happiness of seeing your children grow wholesome through religion, the natural and exclusive capacity of women to give tenderness to their children, the male's responsibility to respect and not touch the pure flower of womanhood until he has been united to her by a priest in holy matrimony and many other, similar sermons. But nowhere did it tell us how to make love.

As most middle-class adolescents have had to do from time immemorial, we then looked for some alternative to our family as a source of information. I went to Tina Berríos, "a boy's best friend" as the boys had nicknamed her, and Andrés went with his friends to a movie of the Shriners from the United States. Our terror of Communists and Masons included the Shriners, who, according to what we were told, belonged to a secret and dangerous sect, but our need to find out about sex overcame our fear.

Andrés came back from his initiation rite quiet and upset and wouldn't share what he learned. I came back confused from what Tina had told me, because besides having kissed a boy and touched him "there," she had not done anything else.

It was then that our morbid curiosity about sex began, and it became even more morbid when we started to buy magazines and romances in English about sexual relationships, and a newlywed substitute math teacher arrived in our school and two months later she was pregnant. Therefore she had sex with her husband, that was the proof. So she was not a virgin anymore. Did it hurt? Did they take off their clothes? Did they see each other naked? How did they do it? Like in the movies? Did they turn off the lights because they felt ashamed? Or did they keep them on as I dreamed I would so I could see what men really had there?

Suddenly, all the men's briefs which were hung out to dry in yards and verandas in Santurce were of special interest to me because they retained the shape of men. All Jockey briefs had the shape of men. All of them, even Uncle Sergio's and Andrés'. Suddenly we were all sexual beings. It was terrible. Was it sinful to think about this? Was it a sin to notice that between all men's legs hung their, their, their, Andrés said "dick," Mami said "pipi," the aunts said "that," Mamá Sara "the birdie." Uncle Sergio never mentioned it. And just then, Auntie Rosi became pregnant, like Margara, like the substitute teacher, everybody was making love and I wanted to know how it was done.

That year could only have been more horrible if it had been longer. I began to gain weight. I got acne and my hair, which had always been beautiful, turned curly and oily, and I would no longer look at myself in a mirror. Andrés grew more and more distant from me, and we only talked about "That" during Holy Week. Again I did not receive communion, avoiding it the first Friday of the month by saying I had made a mistake and had eaten something before going to mass. It was important to have an empty stomach when God entered our bodies. Mami told us that when a person threw up just after communion, a priest had to search in the vomit for the pieces of the consecrated wafer and eat them. It was so Sacred and Solemn! Maybe you could get away without going to communion throughout most of the year, but on Easter Sunday all Catholics had to receive communion under penalty of sin. On Holy Wednesday, before the general confession in school, Andrés and I plotted.

"Are you going to confession?" he asked me.

"Yes," I said, "and you?"

"Yes," he answered.

"Will you tell everything?"

"Of course."

"Everything, Everything, EVERYTHING?"

"Yes, what the hell!"

"Don't talk like that," I corrected him. "I mean everything, even about the books, the movies, what you do . . ."

"What do I do? What the hell do I do?"

"You know."

"Go to hell."

"Don't talk to me like that or I'll tell Mami." It was the only thing I could come up with.

"Listen, I'm a man. Get it? Priests are men. They understand. I can tell him that I bought books about sex, even that I masturbated, and they will ask me how many times, send me to pray a few Hail Marys and I'll be forgiven. But you . . ."

"What about me?"

"You're a woman and you're not supposed to do anything. Women have to be pure. You'll never find a boyfriend, you'll never get married if you aren't pure. The priest won't like it if you know about sex, look at magazines or do anything. He might even tell Mami and Aunt Ele."

My entire world came tumbling down. Andrés was doing me a favor by telling me all these things, and they were true. Men, who had "the wolf inside," as Sara F. said, sinned because it was unavoidable. Since, unlike men, women did not have the wolf's urgency, women were only vicious by choice, because God had given us the strength and the divine grace to overcome temptation. I was a vicious woman. I didn't want to face up to it, but that's what I was. That's why I felt so different, why I didn't want to share with the group, or have friends, or go to parties. I was a lost evil woman, I wasn't in God's grace and I wouldn't be for all my remaining years, since that very day I went to confession and I didn't say a single word about what I was supposed to, about what I had learned or done, and on Easter I received communion dressed in pink. I sang and celebrated with all the other Catholics in Santurce.

Imitating the Catholic people in the United States we all had white, pink, light blue, and light yellow dresses, wore hats, and carried purses decorated with cloth flowers. We all ate lunch in homes decorated with chicks, ducklings, bunnies and painted eggs and ate egg shaped candies and chocolates. I celebrated, although inside I felt I had entered into the kingdom of evil people, of liars, of those who had committed such terrible sins that they would be excommunicated. Me, excommunicated from Divine Grace. I knew it. I was forever disqualified from the kingdom of the GOOD, the JUST, the PURE, the CATHOLIC, the kingdom of my FAMILY. I was in the same league, perhaps forever, with pariahs, peculiar people . . . along with Uncle Sergio? Had he ever experienced something like this?

The year was shaping up as terrible and finally Mami gave us the bad news. They were going to switch us to another school. Our present school was not as good as other schools. Its teachers were very lax, we barely had any homework, we were going to the best school if we could pass its IQ test. One afternoon they took us to solve math problems, to string together colored wooden oval beads, and to mark "Xs" on multiple choice questions. Two days later we were officially declared geniuses, but this designation didn't help us in anyway since, in our new school, the classes were so severe and we had so much homework that we two geniuses never had time for anything else.

A few days later when I came home from soliciting empty cookie cans from the neighbors, I saw Evaristo in the porch. Four times a year Nati sent us around the neighborhood to look for "clean, empty cans" which we took to Sister Soledad, our cousin, who was a nun living in the convent where they made the wafers for communion and used the cans to send the wafers to the churches.

"Hey, Lidia, you got good test results from the sisters, didn't you?" I didn't know how, but Evaristo found out everything before anyone else on our block. He was the first Cuban to live on our block. He was a merchant who, within ten years, would become a member of the Caribe Hilton, and see the title on his business card change from "Salesman" to "President" of the Western Corporation, an insurance agency which eventually grew into a real estate agency.

"How about coming to work for me at Uestern when you graduate, OK"? Nati couldn't stand him for many reasons, from his being Cuban, a fact she never forgave anyone, to his inability to pronounce the "Ws" in English.

"Do you hear how he says 'uestern' instead of 'western'? They can't even pronounce words, much less write them, and they want to take over the entire country."

When they said "country" in that context they were referring to Puerto Rico, although they explained to us constantly that Puerto Rico was not a country, that our country was the United States. That reference to Puerto Rico as our country was something that slipped out at times and it confused us a lot.

Much to Nati's regret, Evaristo came in the afternoons to chat with Mamá Sara since he and my grandmother shared a devotion to her most sacred things: the Virgin of Mount Carmel, carrier pigeons, and the television program, *The* FBI *in Action*. Evaristo was the first Cuban exile to settle in our neighborhood, but soon there would be more than a dozen since the Flores sisters, Carmen and Caridad, rented rooms to new arrivals and were soon running a small boarding house.

Evaristo talked about how things were not going well in Cuba, how soon they would shut the door to all who believed in democracy. Fidel Castro had gone from the hero we had all imitated when we played with black and red armbands that read "July 26 Movement" to an abject and evil person because he was a Communist.

He was the first person in our childhood to switch categories from Good to Evil; later many more would switch, most of them taking a reverse path. I listened to Evaristo speaking with Mamá Sara while I amused myself by drawing ancient monuments copied from books. "We'll give Castro a lesson," Evaristo dreamed happily. "When Andresito joins the Army, he'll help free Cuba, right Andresito?" Andrés hated to be called Andresito, but he was so easy going that he didn't complain.

Lately Andrés had been looking sad, and he was more willing than I to be taken out of our school because he'd always had problems there, not with the teachers but with the other students. This semester he was doing poorly in his classes because his classmates teased him. They called him "girl," although he was not queer or effeminate, but he was gentle and didn't like to fight and they dared him and teased him to humiliate him. Mami knew something about it, but not everything that was going on because adults never realize how much schools mirror the real world. There was one group of boys with power, power that no one challenged. They copied during exams, harassed the weaker boys, and humiliated everyone they could.

This semester their game was to pull down to their ankles the pants of the weaker kids. The boys gathered in a gang in the alley that lead to the small field at the back of the school, and when one of the weaker boys went by they jumped him, unbuckled his belt, unzipped and lowered his pants, while all of them held him down, laughed, and screamed, "Little lady, little lady."

I believe that I never hated any group as much as I hated them. They were cowards, rats. I wanted to take a machine gun and shoot each of them right between the eyes and watch as they dropped, the boys, the barbarians, the students from Cristo Redentor, with their white shirts red from blood and their maroon pants black with blood. No one challenged them; everyone took it as a joke. I was determined they would never do that to my brother or Quique, although, since Quique was two years younger than me, they didn't bother him.

That's how I became Andrés's bodyguard, without his knowing it. I remained at school, talking or sitting around the basketball court as if I were waiting for someone, until I was sure that Andrés was safely headed home and had reached the avenue. I knew that one day they would try to intercept him, and I was ready. This made me nervous during the school week. I could only rest on weekends. I, already a vicious and evil woman, was also ready to become an assassin, because I knew that I would kill them, in cold blood, with a silk handkerchief, just like the stranglers from Bombay.

The gang from Andrés's class, with its leader, Chiqui Márquez, decided to attack Andrés on a

Friday afternoon. Fridays are my strong days; I was born on a Friday and every Friday I feel on top of the world. Andrés was walking alone by the small field behind the school. He had accompanied Sister Louise to the convent to carry some chemistry instruments for her. He looked clean; he always kept himself spotless even at two in the afternoon. When he turned the corner, Chiqui and three others came up to him. The one with a pretty face, Manuel Sosa, with whom Aunt Ele wanted me to go to a dance at the Casa de España that summer, was among them.

Manuel said to Andrés, "Come here girl. Look who's coming by. It's the prettiest girl in school." Andrés replied, "Leave me alone. I don't mess with you. Don't mess with me."

"Come here. We have a keepsake for you, now that you're leaving this school for good." And the four of them threw him on the ground.

I jumped up from the court and screamed at them, "Leave him alone."

"Get lost. This is between men," said Chiqui.

"You mean among queer cowards. You're four against one. I'll bet you don't dare mess with him one-on-one?" I said this because all the heroes in the movies said it, and I called them queer because I knew that was the worst possible insult.

"Get lost Lidia. Stay out of it. He asked for it. This is an initiation rite for men. He asked for it by brown nosing and being a weakling."

"And you asked for this," I said as I picked up a stick from the ground and threw it at his face. The stick only scraped his temple, but it was covered with mud and dirtied his face. He was furious.

"Idiot," he yelled at me. "Tomboy."

"Queer, sissy, queer, sissy," I sang to him and I threw a mud covered stone that hit Juan Rafael on the elbow and really hurt. The two of them let go of Andrés, who got up and hit Juan José in the stomach with all his might. Juan grabbed his stomach and could not breath. I approached Chiqui with a stick, wanting to hit him in the face, wanting to see him bleed. I had a holy anger inside me. Andrés continued fighting, I dropped my stick and jumped on Chiqui but he moved and I landed on Manuel. There were kicks and scratches, but since I was a girl they tried to avoid me and not hit me back. Finally the loathsome four ran away. Juan José was crying, and Juan Rafael had blood on his elbow.

We remained very dirty and quiet. We walked back home. I was scared, Andrés was humiliated. If I had been his younger brother, he certainly would have been proud of me. We would have been like the Villalobos Brothers: the Solís Brothers facing the world. But what adolescent likes having his younger sister defend him from his classmates? It was shameful, but nevertheless it was good that he was the only boy who hadn't had his pants pulled down.

As with so many other things that were taking place, this incident left a sweet and sour impression on us: the knowledge that we were vulnerable and could be hurt in the outside world, a place I envisioned as hostile and hateful. I started to think that maybe I was being ridiculous or too weak, but I didn't want to belong to a world like that. I didn't want gangs attacking my brother, or groups of workers telling me that they wanted to fuck me every time I walked by a construction site. I didn't want anything to do with groups, because people in groups became mean. The only useful and beneficial groups were religious groups. I decided that very day to withdraw forever from the evil in people and become a mystic. Go to a monastery. That was it. I'd have a pretty brown habit, a vegetable garden, and a well to draw water from; I'd speak only with God and the birds, like the saints in *Exemplary Lives*.

When we arrived home no one noticed us. We washed our scratches and took off our uniforms before Mami and the aunts arrived. That night they gave us great news: in three weeks we would all take a vacation, first a week in the rain forest, and afterwards four or five days at the thermal springs at Coamo, where they had been promising to take us since we were small. That same night I decided to postpone becoming a mystic, and first see how I fared in life and went to bed feeling calmer, almost happy.

But someone had seen us fighting. Caridad Flores had been walking along Américo Salas Street behind the school when Andrés and I fought with his classmates. The worst thing was that our scolding didn't come right away because that old witch didn't come immediately to tell on us. She waited three days and by then we weren't expecting any problems. Mami called us that evening after dinner and in a very serious tone said, "We've been told that you were fighting in the street."

"They started it first and . . ."

"Shut up," said Andrés.

"That you were fighting other boys like bums, as if you were nobodies, rolling on the ground! And especially you, a young lady! What a disgrace! We didn't bring you up like that, and under no circumstance will we allow this in our family, so you'll be punished, and don't you ever dare do it again."

I didn't argue because I knew Andrés didn't want anybody to know what had happened. As punishment we couldn't go on vacation with the family. This time everyone, absolutely everyone, was going, but since we were punished we had to stay home. Andrés could go only to his swimming class during those two weeks, and no place else, but I was to be locked up in the house for two weeks, without even going to the movies. They were all going to the rain forest and to the thermal springs at Coamo, where they had promised so often to take us, but not the two of us, because we had fought for something we couldn't even explain to them, because even if we tried they'd never understand the need to gain self-respect in the world out there, respect from other people. Since they lived isolated, in an insular family, and not with other people, the only thing that mattered was what other people thought of us; there was no close interaction with anyone not in our family; other people didn't matter, just what they thought of us.

The two of us watched as they made all the arrangements: bathing suits, masks, fins, thermos bottles, sweaters and camping equipment for the rain forest. Andrés didn't care that much, but I cried in anger every night. Now certainly I could no longer be part of that family. Now I would show them. When they returned I would no longer be here. Then I calmed down and thought that at least I would have the house to myself, with Micaela, who would let me do whatever I wanted, and with Uncle Sergio. But no way, they knew better. In order to make sure the punishment was enforced, Mami would stay behind, she was not leaving us alone in the house.

On Saturday morning the three cars gathered in front of our house. They were going in three groups: Uncle Roberto and Aunt Sara with Germán, Quique and Roberto; Cousin Germánico and Aunt Rosa with Rosi, Monsi and Angelita; Cousin Eustaquio, Aunt Ele, Nati, Sara F. and Mamá. Everyone was going except us.

I didn't want to say good-bye to anyone. To rub in the punishment further, Sara F. insisted that I go downstairs to say good-bye, but I hid in the chicken house until after they left. When I came out, Uncle Sergio was waiting. He had a bracelet in his hand.

"Look what I found on the street. I brought it for you as a present," he said.

It was the color of gold and I thought it was very pretty. He put it on my wrist.

"Don't worry, don't feel bad; we'll do many things during these days when no one in the house will bother us," he said. I looked at him feeling an enormous urge to cry, but I held back. Then he embraced me like no one else had ever embraced me, stroked my head, and promised me, "One day I'll take you to the thermal springs at Coamo, and we'll go to the pool, and to the natural baths, and into the town where I know people. I'll take you, don't worry."

And I started to cry feeling ashamed of myself because in my family no one ever cried, but I had no defense against his tenderness.

"Come back right away. Don't hang around San Juan."

"Yes, I'll return right away."

Mami gave in, she always gave in, and in spite of the punishment she let me go to San Juan to buy books from the Encyclopedia Pulga, the "Flea Collection," which were on sale. They were tiny, three-inch tall books that sold for ten cents, like comics, and according to Sara F. also "educated" us and made us "sophisticated." For one dollar I came back with *Attila, Escape, the Tartars are Coming! Mohammed, Quevedo, Legends of the King Father and the King Son* and *The Floating Cemetery* by Emilio Salgari which counted as four volumes. I spent my last ten cents on a comic entitled *Blessed Contardo Ferrini, a Saint in Tails*, from the *Exemplary Lives* collection. With one biography after another, we filled our heads with historical facts. This was important for me because during the first years of my life I had difficulty understanding the notion of time. I didn't understand the difference between a week and a month, and I couldn't tell time until I was almost ten. The fact that we are beings who can be placed in historical time was inconceivable to me.

In my first composition, written in second grade, I wrote that Washington, the first President of the United States, fought in Korea. I could not distinguish one war from another, until, with the help of comic books and movies, as I observed people dressed in different fashions, I began to understand the sequence of human time. The first time I realized that history was not only a thing of the past, but that it was occurring in the present at this very moment, was when we were in the cemetery by the sea cleaning the chapel where Papá Fernando and Papi were buried.

The chapel had a marble altar and several times a year — on their birthdays, name days, Armistice Day, All Saints Day, and on the day we had chosen to observe the anniversary of Papá's death (since we didn't know the exact day my father had died), we cleaned the chapel, changed the flowers, lit candles, and replaced the altar covers with clean ones. When we opened the door, we were always met by the awful stench of dead flowers that had been locked in there for months, which I always believed was the odor of death. While my family took care of everything and prayed one or two rosaries, Andrés, Quique and I walked between the graves and sometimes hid behind the monuments to scare each other, but I asked them to go easy on me because the cemetery terrified me, and they agreed.

One afternoon, while we were in front of the chapel, Aunt Ele went back to the car to pick up a broom and a piece of cloth to clean the floor and she noticed that the radio was still on. She was about to turn it off when she screamed excitedly, "The Russians are invading Hungary; the Russians are attacking the Hungarian people with tanks!"

"Now, today, right now?" I asked.

"Yes, right now," she said, and Mami and Mamá Sara went to the car to hear the news.

Then, for the first time in my life, I realized that history was a continuum, not just what had already happened. And I understood that in a few years this invasion would be history, and after a few more years I would be dead and my grandchildren would come here, to my grave, bringing me flowers. In a single moment I understood the dread of time, and since that moment I have been able to measure hour by hour, minute by minute, every moment of my life, knowing that everything is quantifiable by time.

My discovery of temporal and historical reality caused great joy in my family since they had already begun talking about sending me to Boston for some tests — in those days the illustrious doctors and hospitals in the United States were supposed to be in Boston — to see if I had some nervous or cerebral disorder that prevented me from understanding the notion of time. And after that, they showered me with history books and bought me all those I wanted.

I took advantage of my trip to San Juan to go to the chapel on Cristo Street. Next to it was an abandoned garden enclosed so that no one could enter. On Holy Week, when we made the seven visits to the Holy Sacrament, one visit was to this chapel, and kneeling there, I always looked toward the overgrown garden, next to an unpainted, abandoned house, which attracted my eye more and more with each visit. It also fascinated Mami, and she said that one day she would get permission to walk in there. Years later the government would turn it into Parque de las

Palomas and everybody would be able to go inside, but it would no longer be mysterious or forbidden, and therefore, no longer attractive to us.

For a while I looked through the iron gates at the park, and then I returned home with my load of history books. The days of punishment had been boring but bearable. Uncle Sergio had played parcheesi with Mami and me. One day we played twenty-eight games in a row, right through dinner time, but it didn't matter. Since neither Mamá Sara or Aunt Ele were there, and they were the ones that set the routine in our house, we didn't have to stop for dinner, so we played until late into the night.

When we finished, I started to read and Mami talked with Uncle Sergio about Emilio Salgari and *The Stranglers from Bombay*, which they had read. I took advantage of the moment to ask a simple question, "Why are women a source of sin for men?"

"Whaaat?"

"Yes, in these comics from *Exemplary Lives* they say that women were sent by the devil to tempt saints. And what about female saints? Were men sent by the devil to tempt them?"

"No, I don't think you understand; it's an allegory, it's a symbol, like in the comic book about Saint Anthony of Abad, the drawings of women symbolize temptation."

"But, why them? And why was Blessed Contardo Ferrini good because he never looked at women?"

There, in front of their eyes was the irrevocable proof. In this comic with its beautiful drawings, which I kept always, was this blessed man, who had led a truly exemplary life: an intellectual, a good son, a trusted friend, a professor who climbed mountains with his friends and rejoiced in the love of nature and God. To a large extent, his beatitude, which could lead to his canonization as the Saint in Tails — an example to laymen in the world — was due to the fact that he never looked at a woman. And they showed him walking along a street, his eyes looking straight ahead, while beautiful women walked past him.

All the saints had given up women, even those who were in love like Saint Augustine. The married ones abandoned them to become priests, or they waited until their wives died to reach true peace as monks. In our religion complete happiness was never reached with a woman. And I, almost a woman, and in love as I was with the idea of love, didn't understand why. I asked them again, when they were talking about *The Stranglers from Bombay*, why were women bad, why did Eve tempt Adam, why did God punish us by making childbirth painful, why wasn't it as dignified to be a woman as it was to be a man? Why couldn't we touch the Holy Sacrament . . . ?

Mami started to talk about divine grace, about human relationships, and about how those comic books, since they were published in México, were a little old-fashioned. She told me that she would take me to speak with Father O'Mally in the San Augustine parish because American priests could explain things better than Spanish priests.

I substituted Beatus Contardo Ferrini for *The Floating Cemetery,* and it turned out to be one of those books you resist reading but can't put down. It was about Chinese people who lived in the United States and sent their dead home to be buried in China. Ships full of caskets returning for burial in the land where they or their ancestors had been born. That night I didn't sleep well, and the next day when I woke up early in the morning they were all having breakfast. Mami was dressed to go out. They had called her from Juncos because her last surviving aunt was seriously ill. It was almost six months since Mami had gone to visit her relatives, although they had called each other on their name days.

"Now, listen to me carefully. I'm going with Micaela in a *carro público* to Juncos. I'm going with her because I know she'll be needed there to help my cousins because they always make a mountain out of a mole hill. You'll stay with your Uncle Sergio. Don't leave the house unless you go with him. Do I make myself clear? I don't want to hear any complaints when I come back that you did something you shouldn't have done without permission."

We behaved marvelously. I read the entire morning and Andrés and Uncle played chess. Then we made lunch together.

In the afternoon Uncle went into the study and brought out two bags full of small tobacco boxes. They were full of stamps. Thousands and thousands of stamps in small packages or in silk-paper note-books with pockets for stamps. It was Papá Fernando's collection. "When I was a kid I helped Papá with his stamps," he said. "Do you want me to teach you how to collect stamps?" I was not very interested but Andrés was, and from that day on they started to bring the collection up to date. Andrés was fascinated with the English and Spanish stamps, but Uncle Sergio liked the ones that said "Puerto Rico" the most.

"But they aren't as pretty as the ones from England or Monaco," argued Andrés.

"No, they aren't as pretty as those, but they are from Puerto Rico," he said, acting reticent and strange.

We were watching TV at dusk when Mami called. She had decided to spend the night there because it was too late to look for a car. She gave us the same instructions for tomorrow, she gave us the same lecture again, and she commended us to the Virgin and Saint Joseph, the patron saint of OBEDIENCE, she emphasized.

At seven, when we were ready to watch *Rin Tin Tin* on television, someone knocked at the door. Andrés opened it and both of us stood frozen in shock. Don Gabriel Tristani was asking for Uncle Sergio.

Uncle went to greet him as if it were nothing special.

"Excuse me for coming here, at this time. I don't mean to bother you, but I don't have an alternative."

"What's the matter? Come in. Sit down."

"I can't, no. It's Margarita . . ."

"Margarita?"

"She's about to give birth, but it hurts her a lot. Maybe there are complications. I can't get a taxi because it's a holiday."

"Don't worry, I'm coming," said Uncle.

Andrés and I were looking at Uncle Sergio. He was going to leave us alone? We didn't say anything, but he read our minds.

"You can't stay here alone. Get dressed quickly. We're leaving."

We were already dressed, but in our family "going out" was a different activity from "being in the house," and it required different clothing, even if it was just something a little better ironed, or in my case, wearing socks with my shoes, a bracelet, and earrings, and for Andrés, tucking his shirt into his pants. In a second we were ready. Uncle Sergio sent us ahead with Don Gabriel to his house while he went through the alley in front of the house into the Campo Alegre Neighborhood.

In five minutes he arrived in a car to pick us all up. We put Margara in the back seat with Don Gabriel and me, Andrés sat in the front with Uncle, and we dashed off to the Municipal Hospital. When we arrived, they made us wait in a hall. We walked around, talked, went out for a short walk. Uncle took us to the cafeteria to eat sandwiches, and then we returned.

At eleven o'clock at night Margara's illegitimate son was born. They told us he came in the breech position, with his arm in front or something, in a word "a mess," as Uncle Sergio explained, so Margara needed to have a Caesarean. Since we were like family, they allowed us to see the baby. He was long, white, with light curly hair, and he had, according to the nurse, very blue eyes, although we thought they were dark. Feeling calmer and happy, Don Gabriel told us Margara had decided to name the baby Gabriel Roberto if it was a boy. "I'll stay here. Thanks for everything." He said good-bye, giving the three of us a tap on the shoulder.

That night we could not sleep, although we were tired. "When they find out! When they all find out that we had gone with them by car! When they all . . . ," we said the following morning.

"When they all nothing, because we won't tell them," said Uncle Sergio.

"But they'll know anyway."

"Not if you keep your mouth shut," said Andrés.

"You've always been the snitch here," I yelled at him.

And we would have continued but Uncle Sergio stopped us. "You're grown up now." That was ours and Mami's favorite phrase, and we understood that it was true. "It's enough not to say anything about what happened."

Mami and Micaela returned. Aunt Pura didn't die this time. She didn't die for another seventeen years, although every so often she threatened to do so. Instead, three more of her fourteen children died before her. Every time it looked as if she were about to die, all her relatives, in solidarity, ran to help, maybe thinking that if it really happened and they were not by her side, their consciences would not leave them in peace. The same thing happened more or less to all members of our family. We had a strange conflict in our consciences between guilt and pride, and more than once I thought that one day we would all die of an attack of scruples over something that we were supposed to do but had failed to do.

The day Margara was discharged from the hospital, Uncle gave Andrés and me money to buy what was needed for the baby. We planned to go shopping near the house, but we thought that the salespersons would comment about it and might tell Mami, so we went to San Juan under the pretext of buying candy. We bought diapers, tiny embroidered shirts, booties, and a pair of baby sneakers for Gabriel Roberto. Also a set of bottles and a pot to boil them in, and four pairs of animal-shaped safety pins. "And toys," said Andrés, so we bought him a rattle, a stuffed dog, and some small bells.

We didn't know where to take these things. We had not made any arrangements, so very discreetly we walked by the Tristanis's house, but we didn't see anyone and we didn't dare go in. We got home and while Andrés marched inside, I went to the backyard and hid the packages by the basement wall behind the crotons. Andrés went down to the basement, and we used two wooden boards that had been there for years to slide our secret purchases into the basement. When Tamaqui saw us she began to bark.

"Who's there?" Micaela asked.

"It's us."

"What are you up to?"

"Nothing."

"Come upstairs. Your mother heard you arrive and is looking for you." Mami was cleaning the dressers and taking out clothes. She had a bag full of baby clothing, and she gave it to Uncle Sergio when he arrived.

"I heard Margara had her baby. Take this to her," she said.

She could do it! She could do it! She was free to send presents to the Tristanis, but we weren't. So this was the difference between being and not being an adult: the power to make decisions, even some that would not be thought highly of, that was the special province of adulthood, and I was dying to get there. We intercepted Uncle on the staircase and told him where our things were. "I'll go there now," he said to us. "Later, another day, I'll take you if you want."

But that day was a long time coming because a week after they all returned from their vacation, Aunt Rosa had her baby, prematurely. And, although no one ever said anything, we were always left with the suspicion that they all felt God had been unfair to our family because Margara's illegitimate son survived, and ours, who was legitimate, did not.

Our cousin was born too small; we never understood what happened, but everyone feared the worst when he was still in the hospital two weeks after his birth. One day Cousin Germánico called Mami and asked her to go to the religious bookstore in San Juan to buy some appropriate religious prints for the funeral because the baby was dying.

He had been baptized Agustín and everyone said he was beautiful. Mami bought fifty elongated prints that showed baby angels flying to heaven. They were the expensive kind with golden edges. Printed on them was a phrase from the Bible and the name Agustín who "has gone to live with God." Since he was still a baby who had been baptized and had never sinned, without any doubt he went straight to heaven. God had taken him, so Agustín's fate was not as horrible as that of Moorish children — the unbaptized — who never, never, would go to heaven, Nati repeated almost daily. The lesson didn't go unnoticed, and since his death everyone in my family is baptized no later than a week after being born.

What seemed most unjust was that Agustín had died and not Gabriel Roberto. He was a big, strong child with blue eyes. Mami said Margara wouldn't give any clue about the father.

"No doubt he's American."

"No way. I'll bet he's one of those politicians with whom her father is still associated."

"You see how shamelessly she walks around."

"She takes him to the small park in the Condado

to show him off as if he were legitimate.

"Isn't he?"

"Go mind your own business," Mamá said.

"No, he isn't. He's illegitimate," explained Mami.

The illegitimate Gabriel Roberto received lots of pampering from his mother, who took him everywhere. Sometimes Don Gabriel rocked him in his arms in their house, and we carried him the few times we went to their house secretly with Uncle Sergio.

It gave us such a scary and pleasurable feeling to sneak into Don Gabriel's house with Uncle Sergio. We could feel on our necks the hot breath, the heated angry words, the scolding we would get if we were caught in the act. But we could not avoid the altruistic act, the drama, the challenge of accompanying Uncle Sergio, like members of a secret brotherhood, to the house of that Nationalist, of that lost woman, of that illegitimate child — because no one in the Tristani household escaped the wrath and rejection of my family and of the members of my social class — to drink coffee with them, and sit on their porch, a bit fearful but defiant, hiding a little so our faces could not be seen from the street, perched on the edge of our chairs, but sitting nonetheless.

I was such a coward, even worse than the others. Uncle Sergio was not, and Andrés tried not to be one. He would remain staring at Margara for long periods of time, and once, when she went inside to nurse Gabriel Roberto, Andrés followed her. I looked toward the inside of the house, and I saw him standing behind a red curtain watching her, undoubtedly looking at her tits, and I felt embarrassed. More than that, it bothered me that she was nursing, performing a purely motherly function, showing motherly love, and he was looking at her tits, looking and thinking who knows what.

When we left the house I looked at him steadily; he avoided my glance, and I said to him: "I'm keeping an eye on you."

My anger at seeing maternal love and sexual desire intermingled built up for many days. I didn't know where my loyalty lay, with Andrés, Tina, and all of us, youngsters who wanted to find out and experiment with everything in a short time, or with God, religion, the Church, and my family, who believed in pure love, without any need for sex, except for the few moments, in which, probably without saying a word, a new member of the human race was conceived.

The day we buried Agustín, Cousin Eustaquio came accompanied by a young woman, who my cousins, Andrés and I liked a lot, but none of the adults could stand.

"Just what we need, Eustaquio making a fool of himself in his old age."

"A Cuban. She had to be Cuban," exclaimed Nati.

"They're arriving by the hundreds. What they want is citizenship."

But all this was said when there were no neighbors in the house because "these are family matters," Mami explained. The truth is that Cousin Eustaquio, who was about fifty years old, and a confirmed bachelor, had gotten it into his head to get married.

"That's good. He needs someone to take care of him," said Mamá Sara, to whom the idea of a man being alone in life was inconceivable.

"Men don't know how to take care of themselves,

they aren't strong, they need someone to take care of them," she repeated. "Eustaquio had to wait all these years and finally Saint Judas Tadeo, the patron saint of difficult and desperate cases, rewarded him with that young woman. She seems so good."

"She seems so good, but she's a sly old fox," added Nati.

"At least she's white," said Sara F.

"Who knows! What about the relatives she left in Cuba? You have to see the whole family to make sure that somewhere down the line you won't get a colored kid in your family."

"But if she has black relatives that doesn't mean their children will be black, right?" Andrés was studying the laws of genetics in his biology class.

"Also, if someone is only a little black it doesn't matter, right?" I added.

"You stay out of this," said Mamá Sara who was always trying to get me out of their conversations because she thought I was still too young.

"Wait Mamá, let me explain to her," said Nati. And they told us for the zillionth time how the children of black and white parents could never be happy.

"White people won't accept them because they aren't white."

"Black people don't want them because they are whiter than they are."

"It's very sad. Imagine if you had a child with kinky hair. When you wanted to caress its head you couldn't because your hand would get tangled in its hair."

"Also they aren't as healthy because the blood of white people is different from the blood of blacks."

"But what if they both had the same blood type?"

"Even so, when a blood transfusion is needed, it's better to have it from the same race. There's more homogeneity in the blood."

"We don't have anything against blacks. How could we when Baltazara took care of all of us. It's one thing to be together and another to be all jumbled up."

"But María de los Angeles, Dr. Ponce's granddaughter, has a mulatto father and she is white and pretty."

"Yes, but pay attention. She's 'high yellow,' she's not white."

And it was with just that kind of commentary that we grew up, internalizing all the reasons which have been passed down for centuries from generation to generation for why the races should not mix. Everyone gave different reasons, and then they all agreed with one another. Andrés and Quique learned that anytime they wanted to annoy the family they merely had to threaten to marry black women when they grew up.

"You aren't Germans," Nati said. "Germans certainly love black women. On the islands around here you'll find them married to each other."

"And the Swedes like them, too," Uncle Roberto said, "because there they're all so pale that blacks are a novelty."

"But, do they find black women pretty?"

"Well, some are," said Uncle Roberto, and he disconcerted us. We were never allowed to wear lilac clothes because it was something "blacks did" although Mamá Sara wore them because she was always dressed in half-mourning.

"Nowadays it's difficult to know who has black

blood because they straighten their hair and use cosmetics that make them look white. That's why I worry about that Cuban woman."

"Yes, but they always smell like lilac toilet water or talc. They love that scent."

"You know how you can tell if a person is black or has black blood? By the heel. Yes, the heel, Professor Bueso explained to us at the university that blacks have a narrower and more muscular heel."

We checked people's heels, besides smelling them and looking at the colors they wore, to distinguish, yes, to be able to identify different races, although we didn't know why we needed to differentiate between people like that.

But Cousin Eustaquio didn't care about distinguishing races. He married Socorro, and since they never had children, we never found out if she had black blood. Mamá Sara enjoyed their visits because Socorro always brought her desserts she made and told her stories about what was going on in Cuba.

One day the Bermúdez family was visiting with their two daughters, perfectly well-mannered, ugly young ladies. They had come from Mayagüez to attend dances at the Casino. Socorro spoke of how in Cuba, now that Fidel was a Communist and evil person, the pretty daughters of well-to-do families were taken to him to be raped. Ginny Bermúdez said, "Oh, I wouldn't like to live there." Considering how ugly she was, I was going to tell her that she would never be taken to Fidel, when Socorro went on. "But the good thing is that Batista had that scoundrel castrated when he put him in jail."

I didn't get it, at this point. I didn't understand a thing. When they all left, I asked Andrés what "castrated" meant .

"It's when they cut it off a man."

"And how can a castrated man rape a woman?"

"He can't."

"Socorro said so."

"Well, there are certain cases . . ." but he was hesitating and I realized he really didn't know.

We had to turn to friends in school. Two days later I argued with Andrés. "They don't cut it off. What they remove is the testicles. You don't know a thing!"

He didn't fight back. For some time now he had stopped fighting. It seemed that he was in love.

He spent his days locked in his room listening to Pat Boone or Lucho Gatica songs on the radio. He was always well groomed when he left the house and tried to walk straight and upright. He seemed to be going with Vilma Umpierre, a white girl, but we were not sure.

One afternoon, when we went to Pennock Gardens to buy plants, he didn't want to play hide-and-seek among the rows of plants and shrubs where he used to really enjoy getting lost with Quique and me. Instead he remained behind speaking with the gardeners and with Aunt Ele, and when we got into the car he was carrying a plant in full bloom.

"Who's that for?"

"It's a present."

"For whom? For Vilma?"

"Shut up, idiot."

"Be quiet Lidia, don't bother him," said Aunt Ele.

Everyone was happy that he was becoming a young man, and he had selected his first girlfriend well.

I felt that that summer was one of the longest in

our lives, and when it ended, everything suddenly changed. We began our school year at the Academy of Nuestra Señora de la Asunción. Classes were very hard, the homework was endless and it took us all afternoon and part of each evening to complete it. My enthusiasm didn't last long. I realized, that in order to get As, I would have to sacrifice television and comic books, and I didn't want to give up the activities that were my refuge.

My grades began to drop, but Mami made it clear that she would not let us return to our old school.

In September, when it cools down, and "Paris becomes Paris again, because Parisians leave when it gets hot and there are too many tourists, but they return in the fall," Aunt Ele and Nati left for Europe. They sent me lots of postcards because they had decided that it was time for me to start a postcard collection. Andrés collected coins, matchbook covers, and now he had started to collect stamps, but I didn't like collecting anything. So as not to be too disagreeable, I agreed to collect postcards, and I began to keep them in a box I had lined with velvet. All the postcards began "Dear Lidia" and ended "Love, Nati," because we never said "I love you" in Spanish.

Quique hardly ever came over to our house anymore because he was also in a new school, and since Andrés used every free moment to go to Vilma's house, the afternoons in my house became a soliloquy. I talked and Uncle Sergio sort of listened to me. They had tried to find him a job, but he didn't seem to fit anywhere.

"Will you go to the States if you don't find a job?" I asked him one day.

"No, I'll never leave Puerto Rico again."

"And if you have to leave?"

"Then I'll go, but I'll return."

"And if you die there?"

"Child, don't be such a pest," Mamá Sara yelled from the kitchen.

"Then I'll ask to be buried here, and in that way I'll end up here."

"Why?

"Because I'd like to be buried here, I guess. Many times you can't choose where you'll live, but you can certainly choose where you want to be buried. That's how you know which country is yours: it's where you'll be buried."

"Like the Chinese?"

"Yes, like the Chinese from the story you read. I've been in San Francisco. I've seen how the Chinese store coffins, by the hundreds, waiting for the ship that will take them to their home."

Uncle seemed as if he didn't want to live and I felt that way too.

When I realized that I would never do well in my classes again, that I didn't have friends at my new school, that Andrés, Quique and I would no longer play around the house, that life was even more lonely and horrible than I had imagined, that I was becoming fat and ugly, very ugly, I decided that I didn't want to live anymore on this island, and I began to wait for Sophia Loren to take me to live in Italy. In the enormous wooden classroom that was built on top of the school's flat roof and that housed the eighth grade, I waited in vain for Sophia's arrival. Sophia would tell Sister Agatha we were leaving, and, in front of my astonished classmates, without sending word home except for a note to Uncle Sergio in Ape language, we would leave for Italy.

My infatuation with Sophia began with the movie *Boy on a Dolphin*, which I saw eleven times. That a humble woman could marry a handsome American archeologist, and that they could love each other, love each other with such passion — he slapped her face because he thought she had deceived him and afterwards that violent emotion carried them crying to the floor to make love to each other — more than anything caused a tremor in me that I could not explain. I fantasized that Sophia was married to Alan Ladd or Yul Brynner and I would live with them.

On the eve of Aunt Ele's and Nati's return from Europe we cleaned the entire house. Uncle cleaned the outside: the yard in the front, to the right of the house, the small yard almost entirely full of plants that ran along the entrance to the garage to the left of the house, and the one at the back around Mamá Sara's chicken house. Mamá replaced all the small crocheted cloths in the living room and all the ones she used to put on the arms and backs of chairs and the sofa. They even washed the sheer window curtains, and painted the pots with the palm trees which decorated the balcony.

Late in the afternoon, as Uncle returned through the front door, he stopped for a moment to watch as Mamá put the sheer curtains back. He went to the record player, searched for a record of instrumental music, played it, and raised the volume loud enough to be heard outside. Mamá began to hum the music. It was a very melancholy tune, catchy, but sad. I knew that it was Puerto Rican music because every time Mami heard that kind of music she would say, "Good

Lord, how obsessed we are in this country with remembering only sad moments, always negative things, instead of remembering joyful occasions." She said this because in my family they had a passion for happy events and hated nostalgia.

But Mamá Sara went on humming that tune, and Uncle Sergio asked her, "You haven't heard this music in a long time, have you, Mamá?"

"That's true my son," she said as she went on tidying up the house, and then Uncle grabbed her by the waist and asked her to dance. For a few minutes they danced in the living room, and I could not believe my eyes. No one had ever danced in my house. It didn't matter whether it was a party or a holiday, music was played, but no one ever danced; I didn't even know that my grandmother knew how to dance. She went on smiling in Uncle's arms, and I wanted to call someone to come and see, but I was glued to the floor by the music, by them, by the sunlight, the piercing sunlight so characteristic of the afternoons in Santurce, that gave life and strange shadows to houses, and by the music once again.

"What kind of music is that?" I asked wanting to break the enchantment I was not a party to.

"It's a *danza*."

"What's its name?"

"Happy Days," said Uncle Sergio.

"Happy Days? How could something so sad be named Happy Days?"

"Because it's about happy days that are gone," said Mamá as she began to sing, and he joined her. "The joyful days of love will never return to console my poor heart." And in a few seconds the sun set and Mamá was happy.

"I didn't know you could dance Mamá."

"Well, I can't dance to today's crazy music, but *danzas* and *mazurkas*, those, yes," she said. "I taught your grandfather to dance *danzas* too, but he had two left feet. But your father and Sergio, they turned out to be good dancers."

"And Aunt Ele?"

"She did have a little flair."

"And Sara F.?"

"Not at all, not she."

"And Aunt Clara?"

"A little more, but she likes livelier music."   Uncle kept looking at me.

"Do you want to learn?" Uncle Sergio asked me.

And in one of those important decisions in life, torn between trying something new and fearing failure, afraid of turning out like the women in my family, I avoided the situation by saying, "No, what for? No one dances to that music anymore. I like mambos," and I ran away with my pride and with my desire to learn to dance with him, and with the image of the two of them dancing to an old *danza* forever etched in my memory.

"Why do you read the same books over and over, Uncle?" Quique asked on the day they were sewing our costumes for the Halloween dance and we were kept in the house the entire day for endless fittings. Although we had been told to leave him alone, we had gone into his bedroom because he was a little ill. He was lying in bed surrounded by the five or six books he always read.

"Do you have friends in New York?" Quique asked, because we had never seen him with a friend here, although sometimes we had seen him say hello to some men from the neighborhood when we went for a walk together.

"Yes, I do."

"And why don't you have any here?"

"I don't know. You go away, do other things, have a different life . . . When people go to live someplace else most times they become distant from their friends."

"Paar Lajervis. What an ugly name!"

"Laagerkvist," corrected Uncle. "He's a Nordic writer, like this one, Sigrid Undset. The Swedes and the Norwegians should be read; their novels make you think a lot."

"And this one?"

"Miguel Hernández. He's a Spanish poet."

"Spanish? I don't like Spanish poets, only Bécquer," I said to him.

"That's normal; young people like Bécquer. Later on you'll like Miguel Hernández. Give yourself time."

"Well, but not now, not today. Will you come with us for the pictures they'll take before the dance?"

"No, I don't think so. Listen, do you really want to go to that dance?"

"Yes," said Quique.

"I like it because I get to wear a costume, and we can play tricks," I said, for since I was put in the new school, I had not wanted to go to any school dances. I felt strange with my new classmates.

Uncle did not say a word. He had withdrawn into one of his silences. He took a poetry book by Luis Palés Matos, and he asked us if we wanted to hear some poems.

Andrés was looking out the window at the sky facing the house. I said that I did not want to hear any poems, Quique said he did. Andrés just went on staring.

"What are you looking at?"

"The sky, to see a Sputnik."

"You can't see them now, idiot. Only at dusk."

"Yes you can, because they've sent many more up," Quique pointed out.

"Who told you that?" asked Uncle.

"Nati and Sara F," we explained to him. "They've just read an article about the satellites the Russians are putting in space."

"And they let their cosmonauts die," I added.

"What?"

"Yes, that's how it is. There are ultra-sensitive radars that are receiving strange noises, and do you know what they are? They're the heartbeats of the agonizing cosmonauts, because sometimes the Russian satellites malfunction, and since they are Communists and they don't love human beings, they don't care, and they let them die out there," Quique went on to explain with the same tone and theatrics as Sara F.

"Maybe one of those Sputniks has a dead cosmonaut inside," I added.

Uncle was looking at us. "Don't believe everything you read; not everything that gets published in magazines is true. You mustn't be so naive," and all of a sudden he shut up. It was the first time he had ever admonished us like Mami and our aunts always did, and it was obvious it didn't make him feel good.

That evening, when we were ready, we modeled our Halloween costumes for Mamá Sara and the others. I was dressed as a gypsy, Quique as a harlequin, Robertito as a bear, and Monsita as a dancer. Since Andrés and Germán were too old for costumes, they wore jackets and ties. When we arrived at the Casa de España, they made us stand in front of the lion fountain, a replica of one in Granada, to take a lot of pictures — together, separate, making faces, showing off our costumes, placing two fingers behind each other's heads to give one another horns, standing very straight — looking like Spaniards, memorialized as Spaniards for future generations of Solises, white, respectable members of the Casa de España.

Since we were getting older and soon we would be entering society, Aunt Clara wanted Aunt Ele to become a member of the Casino de Puerto Rico, but Mami and Sara F. were opposed. "What you find there is a lot of snobbish people. It's a center of ostentation. The Casa de España is one thing; it's a cultural and healthy place. But the Casino and those other clubs opening now are just places to throw money out the window. We aren't like that," they would say.

They talked about "those clubs" because Aunt Clara and Uncle Roberto had just bought a lot in the new and expensive suburb Santa María, and Uncle Germánico and Aunt Rosi had bought one in San Francisco, and soon they would build houses on their lots, because now, according to Aunt Clara, everyone was moving to the suburbs because they were prettier. The San Francisco suburb, however, was sure to be spoiled because Muñoz Marín had bought land nearby for building public housing.

"Everything is sure to go wrong now. The people from the projects will damage property. We'll have burglaries," predicted Nati.

"Don't exaggerate," Uncle Roberto would say. He was a member of the Popular Democratic Party and an admirer of Muñoz. "They have to build projects so that poor people can live near their jobs. They're opening many factories around there, and the workers need places to live."

"But it's not fair to build them next to the suburbs of the well-to-do. He's doing that to see if something good will rub off on those people, but you know that's not the way it works. Since the beginning of time, the only thing that has rubbed off is evil. The bad habits of all those good-for-nothing kids is what rubs off on the kids of the good families that move there."

"Will we move there?" I asked.

"No, of course not, at least not now."

That is what they said, but since Aunt Ele had also bought a lot — to speculate she said — the possibility of moving was always present. I wanted to move from our old wooden house to a new house without creaking floors, where no one could hear you approaching, with air conditioning in the bedrooms, with new, colored bathtubs and not this old ugly white one with four legs, with an electric stove instead of our gas stove, with tile floors and no termites in the closets, and with "Miami" windows instead of ugly shutters. I wanted modern furniture like people had in Doris Day movies. I wanted to leave that old house, but the unknown world of the suburbs scared me.

"And if we move there will those poor people rob us?"

"No, they'll do nothing. Don't pay attention to your aunts; they get hysterical when they have any chance to attack Muñoz," said Uncle Roberto laughing.

"Oh yes? And what about what Papá used to say? We must be careful, Papá said it before he died, Muñoz wants to lead us towards independence because he is a Communist," said Nati.

"I don't think he is," said Mami, "but he is Neo-Malthusian, that's for sure.

"What?"

"Neo-Malthusian."

"Is that bad?"

"That's obscene," Mami said sententiously.

I looked it up in the dictionary but I never found it. Later on I understood that it had something to do with elections and not being Catholic, but it took me many years to understand why being Neo-Malthusian was an insult in my family.

"But are we moving to the well-to-do people's suburb or not?"

"We'll know soon."

"Are we rich now?"

"No, but we aren't poor either. We are middle class, but the educated middle class, not the other."

"Well, we aren't rich, but we'll be," said Uncle Roberto. "You'll see, if you work really hard and use this," and he pointed to his head, "we'll be rich."

Our wealth would come from the latest idea Aunt Ele brought back from Europe. There Nati and she had figured out a new business: to import German toys and Christmas ornaments. Soon boxes and more boxes began to arrive, and we would go pick them up at the docks in San Juan. Then we would go to the Customs House, which I thought was the most beautiful building in Puerto Rico, and from there we'd return home to open all the boxes, from which emerged Hummel dolls, sets of soldiers that seemed magical because they moved along paths on boards drawn along by magnets underneath, remote control cars, and stuffed bears dressed in Tyrolean clothes. We placed all of them on Papá's two large bookcases — which Aunt Ele had painted indigo blue and taken to her office — where they were admired and purchased by her patients. There were toys, Christmas ornaments, angels to top Christmas trees, and even Christmas candles.

From one visit to the next, the patients would order the ornaments and toys they wanted, and Andrés and I would keep records in books just as they had taught us. From the German boxes we learned to write the number seven with a line through it. We loved this because it seemed exotic, and soon we incorporated it into our writing. Andrés was saving money because it had already been decided that he would study in the United States when he finished high school. He did not know what he wanted to study, but everyone said engineering, and we all approved because he was good at math and because it made sense in those years of fat cows, as Aunt Ele would say.

They also decided that it was time for us to learn to drive. My entire family had been taught by Dr. Von Schulow when Nati worked for him before the war in the Department of Tropical Medicine. They used to tell us that this was why there had never been a car accident in our family. As kids we would climb into the car one by one and sit in the back and were only allowed in the front when our feet could reach the floor. We always owned a massive Oldsmobile, and if the heavy doors were not slammed they did not shut completely. We learned to close the doors with such a bang that years later when small compact cars arrived on the island we were a menace to our friends' small cars. We locked the car doors and never spoke to the driver, because the driver was not to be distracted. For the same reason we could not have any ornaments hanging from the car's mirror or any school stickers on the windows. Anything that obstructed the driver's vision or distracted him had been declared unnecessary and dangerous by Dr. Von Schulow. They wore white cotton gloves to drive. These had the dual purpose of improving the driver's grip on the wheel and of helping the driver make clearly visible traffic signals. A hand in a glove is more noticeable, Dr. Von Schulow had explained, in that ancient time when cars lacked turn signals.

Andrés quickly absorbed the German lessons, and in no time he was driving. Sara F., who was the best driver in the family, would take us to an area near Isla Verde beach to practice. I never learned well because I could only keep the car in a straight line when it was in reverse. When I went forward, the hood ornament confused me, and I could not go straight. More than once it looked as if I was about to crash into one of the palm trees that grew along the roads where we practiced. Sara F. decided to wait one more year to teach me.

Christmas time was coming soon and Mamá Sara wanted to paint the house. Aunt Ele was not sure about spending all that money, which would be wasted if we built a new house. They were speaking about that one night when Uncle received a long distance phone call. It was the first time a friend had called him, and everyone went on talking while they tried to listen in on his conversation from the dining room. When he finished talking to the man, he went to his room without saying a word.

This happened again two or three times. We did not know who called him because the operator would only say, "Phone call for Mr. Solís."

And then he asked to see the photos. He asked all of us to look for all the family pictures we could find, and he proceeded to look at them over and over again. Aunt Ele, Sara F., and Aunt Clara had the most. And Uncle Sergio started to organize them, to make copies of the very old ones, to have his favorite ones enlarged, and to write the names of people on them and the approximate dates when they were taken. The most recent one of him was one he had sent us from New York. It showed him on the roof of a building with his foot on the building's edge, posing like an actor, and although it was only two or three years old, it was already prematurely faded.

"We have to take pictures of the house in case they knock it down," he said. "We have to prepare a family tree," he told us, and Quique and I tried to, but although everyone promised to look through their papers for the birth or baptismal certificates of our grandparents, uncles, aunts, and relatives, they never did, so we could never complete it. I sketched the house to make a painting later, but I never finished it.

The phone calls from his friend became more frequent, and he looked harassed, but since I stood by him, I understood that if any problem came up we would help each other. My life centered around Uncle Sergio in those weeks, and they had already found him a job for next January so finally everything in my family was fine and calm. I felt at ease, although he seemed a little nervous.

More than once I noticed that he rushed upstairs from the basement. I knew he liked to sit alone down there and think, without anyone bothering him. Since I used to enjoy being alone down there, sometimes to ponder, but mostly to search for Negri's bones, it did not surprise me. Sometimes I spied on him through the gratings of the wooden air shafts at both ends of the basement. During those moments I felt happier than ever. He was indoors at his most intimate moments, and outside in the garden I felt close to him, although he did not know I was present. Especially on Sundays, when we left for mass, I knew he took refuge in the basement. He sat on some boxes and caressed old Tamaqui. At times he sighed and would swing his legs back and forth, a gesture they always told us not to do, but a movement that you always learn, that is so natural and comforting that you never forget it. I stopped waiting for Sophia Loren and replaced her in my daydreams with Uncle.

I should have known better. When you are finally happy, you like to feel the world has stopped, that nothing will change, that life is a fairy tale, that you will live happily ever after. It was Sunday, and instead of going for lunch with the entire family to La Mallorquina, I returned home to work on a composition I had to hand in on Monday — five-hundred words about the meaning of sacrifice during Advent. I walked in through the back of the house, and I was heading upstairs towards the veranda when I remembered that I had forgotten to tell Micaela to prepare the soup for six o'clock because Uncle Germánico was coming for dinner. I went down into the basement and entered on the right, to the area where we kept the dogs tied during the day, and I turned left towards Micaela's room, but before I could call her I heard sounds — sounds as if someone was tired, panting, or laughing. Then I felt the fear of discovery, that purple, almost blue, fright, hidden and guttural, that feeling you have when you know you are about to discover something you don't want to know, and I looked into her room.

On the bed, naked, was Micaela, and Uncle Sergio, dressed, was lying on top of her. They were kissing, sweating like crazy, hugging, sort of tossing, I don't know what they said because I could not hear, although I knew what was happening. Were they in love? Did he love her? That was my main question, because I could not imagine making love without being in love. At thirteen you do not want to imagine it. All of a sudden Micaela got up, and I jerked back terrified, realizing that they could see me. I hid behind some boxes, but I could not see inside the room from there. I heard her say: "It doesn't matter. It's nothing. Even if it happens often, one day it won't happen. I'll go upstairs now in case someone returns and comes looking for me."

And I smelled a cigarette. I waited to hear her steps going upstairs, and then I peeked into her room. There, in a room that smelled of lilac toilet water, tangled in damp sheets, was Uncle Sergio, looking towards the ceiling, immutable, breathing heavily, but in absolute silence, sweating, disturbed, defeated.

I don't know how long we remained like that, both of us lost in our thoughts. Later he sat down, he ran his fingers through his hair; I hid behind the door, and he walked out slowly. I heard him go upstairs, and I went into the room. I could not take my eyes away from the bed, from a real love-bed. I got close, and I touched the sheets; I looked out to see if some-one was coming, and then I ran and laid down on the bed. I tried to smell the pillow, but it smelled only of lilac water. There was hair on the bed and on the pil-low. It was a mess and I curled up holding the pillow tightly.

At that moment I thought I heard a door open, and I jumped up and left the basement. I went out into the scorching midday sun, I walked by the side of the chicken house and sat behind it facing the rabbit hutches. Suddenly I remembered I had my Sunday best on, and that my clothes would get dirty. I got up, but I could not avoid feeling even more than surprised — suffocated. Then I heard Micaela calling me. I went out by the gate, walked towards the driveway, and answered from there.

"Your mother's on the phone. She wants to know if you're all right," she said.

"Of course I am. Why wouldn't I be?"

"Well, she wants to know if you arrived OK. She says they left the church over an hour ago, and I told her I hadn't seen you."

"Tell her that I got here O.K.," I answered with impudence, upset with their keeping track of me as if I were a five year old. I came up to the house.

"Where were you?" Uncle Sergio asked, still looking a little unsettled.

I looked at him for a second, then lowered my eyes, and I said "Around here," emphasizing "here."

"Are we going to eat lunch?"

"No, I don't want to."

I went to my room. That afternoon I planned several ways to kill Micaela. The one I liked most was to drop a hammer from the second floor as she was walking by so that it would fall on her nape and kill her instantly. I also thought about confronting my uncle, about squealing on him, about humiliating him in front of my entire family for going to bed with a maid, with a woman that used lilac water. Sometimes I felt that I hated him intensely, that he was a dirty old man, vile, like all men, because he could not be in love with her, he could not.

And I could not write the composition, I did not even try, because everything inside me hurt, everything. Although I did not cry at all, I felt as if I had cried all afternoon and evening. The next day I told Mami that my throat hurt, that I had a fever and I couldn't go to school. Mami felt my forehead. "There's no fever, forget it. Go. If you can't stand it then you can come back, but at least you go and you hand in your composition".

"I didn't write it."

"What? Why?"

"I couldn't, that's all. I couldn't. Don't you understand? Sometimes you just can't."

"Where there's a will there's a way. There's no use crying over spilt milk. Young lady, don't you come to me with stories." When they started addressing me in this formal tone, I knew there was no escape.

"But I don't want to go to the nun and tell her I didn't do my composition. She'll scold me."

"And his mother said to Boabdil, the last Moorish king of Granada, 'You cry like a child over what you did not know how to defend as a man.' If you didn't do what you're supposed to, don't be a coward. Don't pity yourself now. Get dressed right away, go to school, and face whatever you have to face."

Uncle Sergio was helping Mamá Sara to remove the mosquito netting from the canary cages, and he looked at me without saying a word. Our eyes hardly met. I got dressed, I dragged myself to the bus stop, I arrived at school, I waited for the third period, and when it was my turn to hand in my composition I said very softly, "I don't have it." The sister did not say a word. She simply marked an "F" in her roster. If I could have, I would have explained to her that the only things I could have written about that day were the feel of damp sheets and how to kill someone.

When I returned home I wanted to explode, but

there was no one to confide in, there was no one, no one. For years to come there would be no one. You are never as alone as when you are an adolescent and have a secret; you are never in as much pain, you never feel as torn inside as you do at that age, when, instead of growing up you are falling apart. I wished for a war, a catastrophe, a storm, some bloody incident, a fatal car crash in front of my house, anything, which would help to release and burn up all the anger and surprise I carried inside. There was no war, no collision, no catastrophe that day. But ten days afterwards, a bloodless event would contribute to my becoming even more unsociable and introverted for the next few years.

A Wednesday, the 8th of November, at 5:41 in the afternoon, the white ship Bohéme thundered its horn to signal its departure from San Juan harbor. American and German tourists, chubby and red-faced like strings of little sausages, marched on board from the dock at pier nine. And among them, walking slowly, and carrying a suitcase full of the books he always read, cowardly fleeing from Puerto Rico, was the only man I had ever learned to love. I looked only at the length of the ship and the contrast between the blue sky and the black, yellow, and red stripes of the German flag it flew. From the small square in front of the post office where I stood, I refused to lift my hand and wave a handkerchief to say good-bye to Uncle Sergio. I even refused to look when the ship sailed out of port. While everyone was watching the Bohéme, I turned and looked at the Customs Building, pink, beautiful, and deserted.

No one talked much on the trip back home. Only Aunt Ele, who was driving, spoke once in a while.

"Yes, let him travel, live in other places. That's the best thing in the world, to know other places, and there he has a great job, Mamá."

I was thinking all the time of that afternoon two Sundays ago, and the following Monday night when Uncle Sergio called Quique, Andrés, and I and told us, cryptically, that he had to return to New York. I wanted to scream at him that he had said he would never leave, but I kept quiet. Then he distributed his belongings between us. He gave Andrés his stamp collection, Quique his compass and a Spanish art book, and me his painting case and a book about Matisse I had never seen before. I wanted to fight with him, and I remembered Mami comparing me to Boabdil: I did not want to be a coward, but I had no weapons to fight him.

When we got home the day Uncle Sergio left, I went for a walk in the backyard to try to understand how it was possible to have your life cut in half, changed so much in just three days, in just one day, in an instant. I went to the basement. I was thinking of burning down Micaela's room or letting the dogs loose there to make a mess. I sat on the box Uncle Sergio used to sit on to dig in the earth, but nothing made sense to me. It was not until the end of the school year, when they asked us to read George Bernard Shaw, that I would find the first clue to decipher the sadness I felt. It was a quote I would write in the margins of every page, on the book marks I made, and I would place it as a scapulary over my bed: "When you learn something, at first you feel as if you've lost something."

I want you to know that before you arrived I could clearly identify the scents I liked best, the smells that fulfilled my needs and ordered my life: the smell of crayons from my childhood and school years; the smell of coriander from daily life; the smell of gunpowder from the firecrackers of my games and Christmas holidays. Then I began to like your scent, and it went hand-in-hand with the smell of books, particularly art books, and I have never been able to separate them. But when you left they cleaned your room, and there was no trace of your scent. No matter how much I searched your closet, your bed, the corners of your room, I could not find it. And they took your hamper from the bathroom and left no trace of you there, either. So, without your presence in this house, without the Apaches of the Night, with no friends, I took refuge in school, in comic books and movies, and in everything that carried me to my fantasy world.

And the most beautiful thing that arrived in my life then was literature, entirely in English, which convinced me even further that English was my true language, the everyday language you used in New York. In school they asked us to read many European novels, translated into English so I came to know English better than Spanish. While the harping of my Spanish teachers kept Spain's Golden Age literature foreign and removed from me, the nuns who taught us English made literature something alive and familiar.

The nuns were educated, in love with their language, and dressed in black — austere virgins of Notre Dame — with bands of white framing their faces. All of them had pink skin; they were the pick of the American nation. It was said that one of them was a relative of Grace Kelly, from such a rich family that her father sent thousands of dollars every year so that the school could buy velour paper in every color so that we could have the most beautiful bulletin boards in all Puerto Rico and the best laboratory and audiovisual equipment. But everything was given, received and thanked for in English, from our grades to our prayers; and we learned to think and feel in English, and to distance ourselves more and more, some forever, from Spanish.

They educated us well, Uncle, very well. Together with Uncle Tom's Cabin came an explanation of civil rights and racism in the United States. Portrait of a Lady was accompanied by a lecture about women's liberation. Almost all the nuns were Irish, strong, perhaps genetically revolutionary, if not vocationally. They educated us to be concerned Christians, socially responsible, and liberal, having as our guiding light and model the first Catholic President, John F., Kennedy, and his wife, who was so educated that she spoke French. I devoured all the books they gave us and the music they played for us by a trio named Peter, Paul and Mary that sang about brotherhood among people. I submerged myself in everything that allowed me to escape who I was and what I felt.

That sad Christmas after you left, they asked us to write an essay about Longfellow's poem "Evangeline." We had to read about its poetic structure, cadence, cultural and historical contexts, and write a twelve page essay over the Christmas vacation. We went for a week to El Yunque tropical forest, and I was walking up and down the trails carrying the poem, reciting it in the rain forest, certain that in such environment, inside the woods, I would come up with the most clever and poetic essay. I walked the paths in the rain forest trying to find some inspiration, but I could not discover it. As I whispered "This is the forest primeval, the murmuring pine and the hemlock," I was sweating like crazy because I was in the middle of a tropical forest, and already by eight o'clock in the morning the mist and cool morning dampness had vanished, and instead of pines there were prehistoric palm trees and gigantic ferns, a tropical forest in the wildest, truest sense, foreign to what I was reading and to what I wanted to be, foreign to what I had to study and analyze, but nonetheless mine, more like me, since I sweat so much, and more familiar to me than the whispering woods of the suffering Evangeline. And it bothered me. And what bothered me most of all was not being able to translate "primeval," because in Spanish it was something like "primigenio," which did not sound poetic.

I became more and more frustrated in those years, while you took refuge again — see, rumors did get back here — in soliciting money on the streets for causes, in attempts to study and conspire, in friendships with undesirables, in the poems and poetry readings of Miguel Hernández, Gabriel Celaya and Luis Palés Matos, in causes, accepted more out of habit and familiarity than out of a true conviction for fighting, because people get tired of all things if they have no faith, and you, I already knew, barely had any left.

I was often frustrated although I had productive spells. The nuns made me join some clubs because we all had to develop social skills and learn to work in groups. I aspired to the Honor Society, which represented academic and moral excellence, but I soon realized that its members were false representatives of honor. They cheated on exams and later paraded in front of us with their awards and ribbons as if they were truly exemplary. I rejected them and joined the least important, the most nonacademic club: the poster club for school campaigns. There I found my true self, exploring with colors, a true heir to the Fauves, savage inside and out, painting pictures of animals picking up garbage for the school clean-up campaign, or the chests of carrier pigeons crowned by halos for Lent.

In all else I was a scholastic disaster — although I was respected in drawing and history — and finally by the time I began high school, I managed to gain some self-respect.

I also tried to be good, almost stoutly devout, to go to mass everyday in order to purge my absence from God. I was never able to love the Virgin Mary because I had nothing in common with her, as I had with the other saints, especially the ones that were active and did things like Ignacio de Loyola, Augustine and Francisco de Borja. My religious piety elevated itself to the rank of mini-inquisitor, as Sister Claire put me and three other girls in charge of censoring the Paris Match magazines which we used for French class.

We had to cut out all the breasts so that they would not provide the boys with a temptation to sin. The sister explained to us that if this were a girls' school, we would not have to censor the magazine because the sexual material it contained was only attractive to boys. We had to remove the advertisements for bras, slips, and revealing bathing suits. Also the ads for nightgowns, because we had to study French from a Christian, pristine, and filtered Paris Match, without any sign of tits. Seated, each of us armed with a pair of scissors, we scrutinized every page of the French magazine, moral censors at the age of fourteen.

How could we have turned out differently? I know you left here believing that the three of us had something of your rebelliousness. How could we have grown up to be something different from what we are now: uncertain, doubtful, incapable of knowing what to do, how to think, to whom to dedicate ourselves? How could you have deserted us, left us to grow up like this? Did you feel free of guilt? Didn't you know you also had a responsibility to give continuity to what you had begun, our complicity, our awakening, our attempt to fight for our identity? Or is it that your identity was still unclear, and you hid that from us? One can't just arrive and ignite ideas and feelings in a person and then all of a sudden leave and turn them off. And that's what you did.

And when the crucial time arrived, the moment when adolescents are captured forever with myths, the Spanish teacher talked to us about epic heroes. She told us that each culture has one, the archetypal who represents its accomplishments and failures. She compared for us the Greeks and the Trojans, El Cid, Roland, the Valkyries, King Arthur; she explained to us that being heirs to Hispanic culture, our hero was El Cid. But it wasn't true, Uncle. I was never moved by that austere, irreproachable man, like my grandfather a warrior of rigorous honor, a father of two daughters captured and humiliated, a story I detested. I adored King Arthur and his knights, the sad Gareth of Orkney, and Galahad, the most tender and pure of all men, and Excalibur, the sword . But above all, I knew that my hero was Arthur, who failed in his quest, the wise man, dead without reason, mourned by the queens dressed in black, his body traveling in a boat that floated down a river clothed in mist.

The legend of the king defeated by death, of the most noble kingdom that ever existed, nobility that still lives, captured me a thousand times more than El Cid, and forced me to confront myself. Why aren't I what I'm supposed to be, and why don't I like what I'm supposed to like? I don't like opera, I like mambo and merengue; I don't like French, I want to learn Italian; I don't want to memorize the names of the Greek gods, I want to memorize the names of the Aztec and Inca gods. I never learn what I'm supposed to learn. I never manage to adapt myself. Why don't you come to talk to us, to help us leave this island?

One day I went shopping with Mami to Old San Juan. There was talk that the old city was going to be renovated, but it was as dirty as ever. After having our ritual snack at the cafeteria in González Padín Department Store, I leaned against one of the display windows facing the Plaza de Armas while Mami went to buy lottery tickets. I looked across the square at the dirty and peeling Town Hall. Everything was so abandoned: the two fountains had been dry for years; filth, dust, the winos sitting under the trees, the decayed statues of the four seasons waiting for better times. The heat bothered me, and the town, and the island, these annoying afternoons, these trees that grow without any desire to do so, this feeling of smallness, of not having one single square like the ones in Paris, one single landscape like the ones in Switzerland, these balconies, these cobblestones, these dead leaves on the ground, this belonging to this dirty country.

Why don't we have anything of value, Uncle? Why don't we have a single worldwide famous artist, a poet, a painter? And not that painter, Oller, whom you mentioned to us once. He's not even in art books. Not even a saint? People say that Saint Rosa de Lima was born here, but she's Perú's patron saint. In the series Exemplary Lives they've presented dozens of famous people from all over the world, from India, Argentina, the United States, Sweden, France, and never one from Puerto Rico. On dictionary flaps they put the flags of all the countries, even one of the International Red Cross, those of the British Colonies, and the Virgin Islands, but ours is never there, because we aren't anything, not a country or a colony or a commonwealth like the British islands. We're nothing. We don't exist. We are shit, I thought, and I don't want to belong to this country!

I had these fits very often, but without realizing it, I was becoming more civilized, that is, accepting things as they were. My family promised me a trip to Europe the summer of my junior year, if I did well in my classes, as they had already given Andrés and Germán. I accepted as long as it included Rome because nothing else interested me at that time.

Thus I was taken in pilgrimage to the land of our ancestors, because supposedly all our roots were in Europe. Some Spanish cousins seemed to me a bit too dark, but when I returned home and consulted with Andrés, he reminded me that the Moors were in Spain for 800 years, that I should not bother our family with such matters, and I, so civilized and ladylike, did not even mention it.

I traveled all through Europe with Sara F. We went to Vienna to see the dancing horses; we saw the midnight sun in Norway, Hamlet's castle in Denmark, we sat at the cafés in Paris, and fortunately no Frenchman ever thought to kiss my nail-bitten hand. But above all we went to Rome. I walked alone through Rome; I took souvenir pebbles from the Coliseum, and like the young women in Three Coins in the Fountain, I threw coins into the Trevi Fountain so I would return, because Rome was the center of the world and I wanted to leave a part of me there. I did not see Sophia Loren, but I knew that one day I would meet her when she was old and everyone else was no longer interested in her. I would invite her to spend time in my New York penthouse, because sometimes I thought I would become a "career girl," which sounded superb, although I could not define exactly what that was. But they all had luxury apartments in New York, and Sophia would visit me and together we would reminisce about how we grew up, and we would marvel at the fact that both of us were born on a 20th of September, and I would have money to invite her, Carlo Ponti, and their two kids to an elegant dinner in New York.

Everything seemed to be under control my first years of high school. With my fantasies I could escape my feelings of insecurity and of being colonized, although I still did not understand *what that meant. I had not even heard of those terms then.*

I *didn't even cry for you. Can you believe that? Because in our family we don't cry over minor things, only when a person dies, and you weren't dead, just gone.*

One day at a party I allowed a boy, Juan Manuel, to kiss me. I let him do it because everyone did so to the tune of a bolero. In *our world, the only window to Latin culture was music, and when we danced* boleros, *we kissed. When I arrived home after drinking two rum and Cokes, and with my mouth full of kisses that weren't the ones I wanted, I began to cry. To cry for you and me and for everything I had never wanted to know. Then I became ridiculous, as Mami would say, and I began to listen to songs on the Spanish radio stations, instead of the English stations I usually listened to. I, who wanted to be like Grace Kelly in* High Society *or Doris Day in* Pillow Talk, I *fell in love with a song that reminded me of you. I don't know why. It went something like ". . . if you die first, I promise you that I'll write the story of our love, the chant of a soul filled with longing. I'll write with blood, with ink-blood from my heart."*

That tacky song, that idiotic, painful, and intensely Latin song, which embarrassed me right up to the core of my assimilation, was my favorite. I filled up my days thinking that one day I would write you and tell you all this. I was going to sketch your picture, to describe you, to show our affection, to tell everyone that I loved you. And then I would think, what for? What if you didn't appreciate my love, if perhaps it was shameful, sinful, and immoral? What value could it have to tell about you and about all my love for you if you didn't even love me as I loved you and if you had deserted me. It would be pathetic, wrong, in bad taste. But I wanted to embroider you in a cloth, to draw you in a book, to paint you with words, to possess you, to duplicate you, and then to let the whole world know you.

As Puerto Rico grew and the most important aspects of industrial culture arrived here, from private swimming pools to elevators without the number thirteen, from escalators to the Swiss Chalet's fruit tarts — "finally we have quality pastries," my family would say — I only thought about you. For the first time since my childhood, I was skinny again. My family had party dresses made for me; they forced me to go more often to my classmates' "get togethers" so that I could mix with people from our same class. And I would look at all those young men and Juan Miguel, whom I never allowed to kiss me again, with their mustaches slowly emerging, as they talked about the cars and the boats they were going to have, smoking like experts under the lanterns on the patio of Doctor Sanabria's mansion, in the Rastrelli's luxurious house in a new suburb, on the terrace of the penthouse of the engineer Silva-Longo, withdrawn in my own world at the parties of my adolescent classmates, where invariably they served hamburgers and potato chips, where we danced too close to each other, where the girls, members of the Association of the Daughters of the Virgin Mary, danced with the boys, members of the Association of Jesus Christ, forgetting that kisses longer than fifteen seconds were a mortal sin, as Sister Mary of the Cross explained to us; where we played at being adults, my classmates, my illustrious incompetents, my mediocre soulmates, who fifteen years later would say with great enthusiasm in the back-to-school magazine that the most important thing that had happened to them the previous year was twisting an ankle playing tennis; my children of Americanized doctors, of Spanish merchants, of new and rich lawyers, I would watch them as they danced and had a good time, solitary witnesses to my inability to socialize, to the complexes and loneliness which would make me leave the parties just an hour after they began, because I was walking around with you inside of me, outside of me, around me, because I was entangled in a spider web, in your web, your scent, your milk, my spider, my temple, my sacred cow, my everything, my relative, my son, my brother, my uncle, you fulfilling everything. When I had to take an exam, I entrusted myself to you, to Sergio, Sergio, Sergio, knowing inside of me, but without yet accepting it, that years later, because life goes on and people have needs, there would be others who would become intertwined in my feelings and in bed with me, others would be lying on top of me, but I would only be under you, always with you, only you inside, only your smell and your truth.

I believe that Aunt Ele was very worried about me in my senior year. It had been decided already that we would move to a new development, and the new house was already under construction. They waited until my graduation to move because I was so thin and quiet they feared a change of this nature would harm me, and I would not successfully finish high school. And just as I thought I had always wanted, we left for our new house, with air conditioners in each bedroom, without creaking wooden floors, without mosquito nets, without hard-to-close windows, without a second floor, with two bathrooms instead of one, with two cars so we could drive around separately and not all together like before, and with a big lawn which we could not step on and which separated us on all four sides from our neighbors.

Villa Aurora was demolished in order to build an apartment building, and Mami warned me not to go by the old house while it was being demolished. I told her that I didn't care, that I wasn't sentimental and would not be affected. She told me that no one should ever go back to see a dilapidated house you once lived in because it moves you deeply, that it had happened to her when she went to see the house where she grew up in Juncos.

As usual I didn't listen to her. One day I got on a bus and got off at Las Villas Street. I walked toward our house, and when I saw it my body froze, a streak of cold welled up from deep inside, from my heart. It was only a shell without a roof, a skeleton. All the walls, doors and windows had been carefully removed, beam by beam, timber by timber, because we were going to build a house in the countryside with the good wood. All the trees, the rabbit hutches, the hen houses, the garage and the back staircase had been demolished. I realized then that I loved it, that it was my home, that I never sketched it and would never be able to visualize it completely, that I would never find Negri's bones, that there would not be a trace of you in this country, that my life had been divided and everything would be measured from now on in terms of the times in the old house and the times of the new house.

Pedro was working with the demolition crew, and when he saw me he called me to show me what he had found. When they began to dig in the yard, where the hen house had been, they discovered wet sand, not soil, a few feet from the surface, just as Germánico had said, because that sector of Santurce had been stolen from the sea. And from the sand emerged whitish, gigantic crabs which Pedro had placed in a cage. I looked at them but they were disgusting. They were the primeval settlers of what had been my home. I looked at Villa Aurora's skeleton for the last time, the towers that were no longer towers, the basement that was no longer a basement, and I ran away. And I needed you so much that day.

When we built the house in the country on the land we had inherited from Papá Fernando at least the wooden front door from Villa Aurora, polished and painted, with its big glass window covered on the inside by a sheer curtain, gave the impression that this was our house. Aunt Ele said it was so sad that you were not there, that you would have loved it because as a child you always loved the countryside, and if you were taken to a farm for a few days, you sang all day long. And then I thought that upon your return I would know all your songs, the ones you never told me you liked because you never talked to us about that, although we knew that you listened with the volume very low to WKVM, the maids' radio station, as Sara F. used to call it.

I sensed that they were Puerto Rican songs, at least Latin, and I decided to learn as many as I could. Do you know how many I learned? All the boleros, all the traditional music I heard on the radio, Christmas songs, the plenas of Concepción and his orchestra, and danzas, all the music that my family rejected because they preferred to listen to Spanish paso dobles and songs from American movies. But I played songs on the living room record player, defending my right to prepare myself for you, until they bought me a little record player for my room so I would take my tunes someplace else. I learned the words of many songs waiting for you, waiting to hear from you, waiting for a letter addressed to me and not to the family, and I saw myself in your photos, in your green eyes, and thought that at that very moment you were looking at someone else, and I would shout at you "You're my family," but it was not true, and I believed I would keep all this inside me forever.

But today during an afternoon of light rain, like the day you arrived, I sat on the patio of this new house without a basement, and I began to dig in a pot where a fern was planted, and the memories rushed back like a scream, like lightning: the first time I saw you, the days you lived with us. I remembered you with all the old tenderness, and I saw you with Micaela, getting up from the wet sheets, dead in the mist like King Arthur, but unlike him, defeated without having had the courage to fight, defeated and leaving behind a myth, and I remembered even more vividly the day you danced a danza with Mamá Sara, that song of old time,"the joyful days of love will never return," and holding back my urge to cry and discovering that I would still go on with my life, I opened myself to you in an uncertain and authentic Spanish, and I grabbed paper and pen and began to write this letter which began, "Happy days, happy days, Uncle Sergio . . ."

My Uncle Sergio never answered the letter I sent him during my freshman year in college. For years we received sporadic and brief letters about his life in New York. Without rushing, but too quickly, Andrés, my cousins, and I grew up. Andrés went to study in the United States, and he took his stamp collection with him. Quique and I entered the University of Puerto Rico. He kept the compass that pointed only south, and he carried it with him every time he went on an outing because that seemed to him the most logical thing to do. I took drawing classes just to be able to reproduce Villa Aurora's facade, but I was never able to remember it. I did not know why Quique and I tried so incessantly to keep alive our memories of the old house. We talked a lot about how we had been and how we were now, and one day, without intending to, because such things can not be planned, we realized that we had grown up to be Puerto Ricans, and that we could not be anything else.

That revelation, which at first had something Messianic about it, lead Quique to wear a Puerto Rican flag pin on his shirt, and me to wear a leather bracelet decorated with the flag from Lares, where the armed uprising against Spain had taken place in the 1800s. Both items were bought at a small crafts fair that a pro-independence group had set up at a beach festival. Our families reacted more with surprise than with indigination to our treason, to ideas, that according to them, the Communists had planted in our heads.

"This surely is the last straw. 'Independentistas' in our family. Papá was so right!"

"So much talk about the flag, the motherland, and you can't even distinguish one root vegetable from the others."

"I'll bet you can't find Moca on a map of Puerto Rico."

"Who was the first Puerto Rican governor?"

That one was easy. "Muñoz Marín," I said.

"You see! It was Piñeiro! They don't even know Puerto Rican history, and they think they have the upper hand!"

It was true that we barely knew a thing about our country, because none of them or anyone else had taught us anything about it. We had lived for so many years locked behind the sweet and sour fence of our family home where everything we inherited from the past was European and everything in our future was North American that we could not know who we were. But our family all knew. They were Puerto Ricans, even more than we were.

For Quique and me, our discovery of our Puerto Rican identity gave us cohesion, it allowed us to place in context everything we had begun to learn, it gave us an identity that was linked directly to our daily life, and for the first time it bound us to people beyond family, and made us brother and sister of a large, extensive family, bigger, wider, truly, our own.

Aunt Ele, Uncle Roberto, Mamá Sara, Mami, all of our family, had never had to question who they actually were because when they grew up there was no doubt, they were Puerto Ricans who had been given a U.S. passport. But their times had a settled, eternal permanence, and changes came only with religious holidays, storms and wars. They, who every other second declared their loyalty to the United States, were less assimilated than we were. For them it was not necessary at all to delineate the boundaries of their identity. For Quique and I it was vital because everything was constantly changing. With all our contradictions, without knowing where Moca was on the map or how to dance a *danza*, we went to study circles, we bought books about Puerto Rican history and poetry, we dreamed of finding Taíno Indian artifacts, we posted fliers announcing marches, and we marched, slowly searching for our Puerto Rican identity.

We had less and less to share with our family and with the old neighbors that they went to visit from time to time. We never again saw the Tristani family, although there were rumors about Margara going to look for Uncle Roberto in his office at Fomento, and it was even said that Gabriel Roberto was his son. Shortly after, the Tristani family moved to Florida, and only after they left the country did I finally understand that the long period of my life that tied me to Uncle Sergio through them was finally over.

On a day that dawned quiet and listless as if a storm were coming, we received a phone call from New York telling us that Uncle Sergio had died. I immediately said to the family: "I am going with Aunt Ele to bring him back," and no one objected.

When we arrived in New York, Doña Martita, the owner of the boarding house where he lived, had already sent his body to a funeral home. When we went to his room to get his things, she told us that he was found dead one morning and the news spread among his friends. Three people came to see him before he was taken to the funeral home: a thin, mulatto man who just went into his room, removed the crucifix Doña Martita had placed in his hands, and replaced it with a tiny Puerto Rican flag; a disturbed, sobbing young woman who embraced Uncle Sergio, and in delicate mime movements removed an imaginary necklace from her neck and placed it around his; and a withered young man of an uncertain age who stared at him in silence for a few minutes and then angrily demanded: "Why did you have to die? Why?" and broke down in tears. Doña Martita asked him to leave because she thought he was crazy.

I resented his friends, the ones who saw him on his bed, in his room, in his reality, and I especially resented the young man who had no right to take my place and ask Uncle Sergio not to die.

There we slowly found the missing pieces of the puzzle Uncle Sergio's life had been. We learned that he had been, if not a fugitive, then almost an outcast. The FBI followed him because he met with a group of Trotskyites to discuss literature. He had worked at factories and warehouses, he had tried to organize labor unions, and sometimes he collected money for the Algerian resistance during the war. Several times he used aliases on his jobs and once he spent six months in the New York County jail for participating in a protest. As we discovered slowly, he had been a pariah, a rebel, and probably a homosexual. But Aunt Ele and I brought his body back here and we buried him in our family grave, because as she said: "It doesn't matter what he was. He is a man who's suffered a lot, and we aren't going to leave him alone in New York, because he is one of us." I then understood a little more about life, and about how much we loved each other in my family.

I did not wear mourning because Mami had taught us that it was a morbid Spanish custom, that true mourning took place in the heart and not on the body, but deep inside of me I felt like wearing austere black for him for a long time and not going around in bright colors, of somehow showing him solidarity with his death. And as a small homage to the dreams we dreamt with him and to everything he awakened in us, I swore that I would never go to the thermal baths at Coamo with anyone, and I never went.

AFTERWORD

Magali García Ramis was born in Santurce, Puerto Rico in 1946. She holds a Bachelors degree in history from the University of Puerto Rico, a Masters degree in journalism from Columbia University, and has studied literature in the doctoral program at the Universidad Autónoma in México.

From early childhood, books were her best friends; in school, imagination and writing were her best allies. In high school she worked for the school newspaper and became its editor in her senior year. Even then, she recalls, her writing was marked by a sense of humor.

Her literary career started in 1971 with the publication of the short story "Todos los domingos" ("Every Sunday"), which won first prize at the Ateneo de Puerto Rico short story competition. The publication in 1976 of La familia de todos nosotros, a collection of short stories, earned her a distinguished place in Puerto Rican literature and membership in what is referred to as the generation of the seventies. This talented group of writers includes Rosario Ferré, Tomás López Ramírez, Olga Nolla, Juan A. Ramos, Manuel Ramos Otero, and Ana Lydia Vega. In this first collection the reader encounters the themes, techniques and style the author favors: family life, a distinct historical setting, social criticism, humor, mastery of dialogue, a preference for first person narrative, and use of the female narrative voice. Her keen sense of observation and attention to detail enable the reader to piece together an intricate puzzle of contemporary Puerto Rican life.

Magali García Ramis has written for several newspapers, journals and magazines, including *El Mundo*, *El Imparcial*, *Avance*, *Claridad*, and *La Hora*. In 1993, *La ciudad que me habita*, a collection of her journalistic essays, was published. The articles included in this collection are organized around a variety of themes which have always been among her favorites, themes reflecting everyday situations and containing abundant social commentary and criticism filtered through the sieve of her humor.

Felices días tío Sergio, her first novel appeared in 1986. She has also published short stories in journals and anthologies, written three scripts for movies and documentaries, and is about to finish a second collection of short stories, *Las noches del Riel de Oro*. She was honored with a Guggenheim Fellowship for the academic year of 1988-89 to work on *Las horas del sur*, her second novel. In addition, in 1972 she became a founding faculty member of the School of Public Communication at the University of Puerto Rico and has taught and held administrative positions there since.

In 1976 when she published her first short story collection, she had already begun work on *Felices días tío Sergio*. Published in 1986, *Felices días tío Sergio* quickly became one of the most widely read and important

Puerto Rican novels. Its appeal resides in the literary mastery displayed by García Ramis and in its highly readable portrayal of intergenerational conflict and change within a representative Puerto Rican family during a time of rapid social and economic transition.

In Puerto Rican literature, *Felices días tío Sergio* belongs to a literary trend that emphasizes historical discourse, in this instance organized around the Puerto Rican middle-class and suburbanization — the suburban housing developments that have proliferated on the island during the last forty years. It is a novel with a strong referential component and one that does not question its reality as a literary text as so many contemporary narratives do.

The novel narrates the education, growth and sexual awakening of Lidia, a young girl and only daughter trapped in the bosom of a 1950s middle-class family, and the evolution of her Puerto Rican identity in the midst of a colonial political experience that conspires to hinder her process of self-realization.

The novel is written in the first person, a narrational technique that is associated with memoirs, confessions, diaries, letters, and coming of age novels (*Bildungsroman*). By presenting an "I" who adopts certain conventions, referents easily recognizable by the reader, the appearance of reality in the presentation of characters and events, and the mediation of that reality through the perspective of a trustworthy narrator — a mediation as important as the story itself — an illusion of familiarity, of verisimilitude, is established in the depicted fictional universe.

The first person narrative is a technique that creates the illusion of intimacy between the reader, the narrator, and the fictional creation. However, this narrative technique leads many readers to create a non-fictional text to accompany the fictional one. Naively, first person narratives have been interpreted on many occasions as synonymous with biography, as if the difference between fiction and reality were to be found solely from the point of view or narrative voice.

Despite the apparent identity between the narrator and the protagonist there are temporal, spatial, intellectual and life experience differences that distinguish the narrative "I" from the "I" in the story. The narrative "I" is generally a reflexive being who relates a story in which she appears as a younger and more innocent person seen through the filter of an older and wiser "I." Experience and knowledge mediate between the two "I's." The retrospective nature of this type of narrative suggests the existing temporal disparity between the time of the story and the time the story is enunciated. This dual temporal perspective enables the protagonist-narrator to anticipate events that lie in the protagonist's future, but in the narrator's past, thus creating an ironic distance between the two. This ironic distance allows Lidia to examine her past with a critical eye.

Dialogue is one of the techniques García Ramis employs to create verisimilitude and to give objectivity to this first person narrative. The absence of the narrator as a mediator in the reproduction of the dialogue of the other characters is a way of emphasizing mimetic representation. In the same manner the direct reproduction of Lidia's dialogues marks the distance that separates Lidia, the child/adolescent, from Lidia, the narrator. Through the technique of having the narrator comment on preceding dialogue the author achieves much of the irony and the humor in the novel.

The beginning of the novel sets a precise historical context: the Puerto Rico of the early 1950s, the beginning of industrialization, the first years of Commonwealth status, the beginning period of the island's Americanization. It is the time of Luis Muñoz Marín (1898-1980), who presided over an entire era of Puerto Rican history, and, as the writer Edgardo Rodríguez Juliá has said, is the leader who has left the deepest mark on the Puerto Rican people.

Even the games played by Lydia and her brother — "playing with American toy soldiers, with Spanish decks of cards" — are reflections of the two cultures that shape their lives. Theirs is a bi-polar world divided between Spain and the United States. The opinions and beliefs of the Solís family regarding religion, politics, culture, sex, fashion, manners and proper behavior dominate a great deal of the novel, and, for them, define Puerto Rican identity. It is a world that chooses to submerge Puerto Rico's African and Antillian heritage.

Into this perfectly ordered, closed, matriarchal universe Uncle Sergio arrives, bringing a new voice, opening and extending the world of Lidia and her brother. His arrival marks a rupture in Lidia's life. Sergio is the first counterpoint the children encounter just as they face their elders' world of prejudices. This moment marks the beginning of their education, a coming of age process that eventually enables them to realize their identity as Puerto Ricans.

As the voice of awakening, Uncle Sergio is given a

preeminent place in the narrative; his importance is emphasized by the title of the novel. In Puerto Rico, where the voice of authority has always been masculine, where authoritative histories struggle to deny Puerto Rican nationalism, where the preference is to minimize Puerto Rico's status as a member of the Caribbean community of nations and its African heritage, García Ramis introduces a new voice, a new discourse: Uncle Sergio, an overt nationalist and a homosexual. Her novel attempts to incorporate into the national spectrum discourse from long marginalized groups — women, nationalists, homosexuals, emigrés.

The character of Uncle Sergio is maintained behind a veil of mystery throughout the novel. The reasons for his surprising arrival are never clearly explained or are the motives for his sudden departure. But, just as Lidia's family presents a Spanish-United States polarity, Uncle Sergio depicts another binary structure, that of New York City-Puerto Rico. New York is the place Puerto Ricans escape to, a refuge from political and social persecution, and Uncle Sergio, a victim of both, flees there. He represents the ambivalence of the thousands who have emigrated but who long to return, even if only to claim Puerto Rico as their last resting place. In this guise García Ramis touches the painful reality of the Puerto Rican diaspora.

Happy Days Uncle Sergio provides an encounter with a single Puerto Rican family which serves to symbolize the larger family of all Puerto Ricans. By looking critically at a past era it helps us understand the values held by an entire generation. It does this through Lydia, the protagonist, who undergoes the painful experience of growing up, sorting out and rejecting many of the prejudices and clichés of her family, and subsituting tolerance and understanding, while at the same time she comes to accept her family, her womanhood, and her Puerto Rican identity. At the close of the novel, the family sends Lydia to New York City to bring back the body of Uncle Sergio for burial, despite the huge gap in beliefs that separates him from them. Through this act, the family both acknowledges Lydia as a responsible person and provides a lesson in reconciliation. This, enables her, at the very moment that she is outgrowing the world her family has tried to impose on her, to balance acceptance of her family with her personal liberation.

— Carmen C. Esteves
Lehman College

The Secret Weavers Series

Series Editor: Marjorie Agosín

Dedicated to bringing the rich and varied writing by Latin American women to the English-speaking audience.

White Pine Press is a non-profit publishing house dedicated to enriching literary heritage; promoting cultural awareness, understanding, and respect; and, through literature, addressing social and human rights issues. This mission is accomplished by discovering, producing, and marketing to a diverse circle of readers exceptional works of poetry, fiction, non-fiction, and literature in translation from around the world. Through White Pine Press, authors' voices reach out across cultural, ethnic, and gender boundaries to educate and to entertain.

To insure that these voices are heard as widely as possible, White Pine Press arranges author reading tours and speaking engagements at various colleges, universities, organizations, and bookstores throughout the country. White Pine Press works with colleges and public schools to enrich curricula and promotes discussion in the media. Through these efforts, literature extends beyond the books to make a difference in a rapidly changing world.

As a non-profit organization, White Pine Press depends on support from individuals, foundations, and government agencies to bring you this literature that matters — work that might not be published by profit-driven publishing houses. Our grateful thanks to all the individuals who support this effort and to the following foundations and government agencies: Amter Foundation, Ford Foundation, Korean Culture and Arts Foundation, Lannan Foundation, Lila Wallace-Reader's Digest Fund, Margaret L. Wendt Foundation, Mellon Foundation, National Endowment for the Arts, New York State Council on the Arts, Trubar Foundation, Witter Bynner Foundation, and the Slovenian Ministry of Culture.

Please support White Pine Press' efforts to present voices that promote cultural awareness and increase understanding and respect among diverse populations of the world. Tax-deductible donations can be made to:

White Pine Press
10 Village Square · Fredonia, NY 14063